ENIGMA SQUAD

The Case of the Tiger on the Toilet

Janet,
I hope you enjoy the adventures!
Free Your Imagination!

[illegible]

The Enigma Squad case files:

#1
The Case of the Old Man in the Mailbox

#2
The Case of the Bike in the Birdcage

#3
The Case of the Tiger on the Toilet

#4
The Case of the Nemesis on the Ninth
Coming Summer 2014

The Case of the Tiger on the Toilet

Brian C. Jacobs

www.EnigmaSquad.com

Excite Kids Press
Seattle, WA

This book is a work of fiction. Names, characters, places, and incidents are products of the author's imagination or are used fictitiously. Any resemblance to actual events or locales or persons, living or dead, is entirely coincidental.

Enigma Squad #3

For information, address

Excite Kids Press
PO Box 2222
Poulsbo, WA 98370

www.EnigmaSquad.com

Published 2012

16 15 14 13 12 1 2 3 4 5

ISBN: 978-1-936672-33-2

Library of Congress Control Number: 2012953871

Printed in Grand Rapids, MI, U.S.A.

Distributed to the trade by Seattle Book Company
seattlebookcompany.com

For my Logan,

I am so proud of you and the steady song in your heart.

Thank you for filling our home with joyful music.

The Neighborhood

The Case of the Tiger on the Toilet

Prologue

"Keep going, AJ! You have to catch him!" I said as I bent over to try and catch my breath. "He is the only clue we've got right now!" I huffed and puffed with my hands resting on my knees as I watched AJ continue sprinting up the hill, chasing after the kid.

Scooter caught up with me but didn't stop; he just gave a breathy, "Come on, Ty," as he continued his steady-paced jog up the hill, following AJ.

I had no desire to keep running up the hill, but I knew AJ had no idea what he was going to do if he did catch up with the kid. AJ was one of the strongest junior-high kids I know, but he was probably going to need Scooter and me both in order to overpower the high schooler.

This was the second time in three days I had climbed this stupid hill, and this time I didn't even have my bicycle with me to at least enjoy the supersonic ride back down!

The hill was so steep that it was much easier to look straight ahead at the road in front of me than to look up and keep an eye on Scooter or AJ. I lifted my head to take a peek every once in a while, only to find that the kid continued to climb higher and higher up the steep, winding street. AJ was in hot pursuit, but both of them had slowed from a sprint to a steady jog. Scooter's pace didn't change, so he began to gain on AJ and the kid.

The kid disappeared around the first large bend in the road, and AJ and Scooter followed. By the time I came around the bend, I couldn't see anyone. The three of them must have been far enough ahead of me that they were already around the second bend in the road.

As I rounded the second bend, I came up on Scooter and AJ, standing in the middle of the street. They had stopped running and were looking up at the old Safari House. The frightening old building stood at the very top of the hill, looking down in envy at all the other houses on Hidden Place. The house had long since been abandoned, and years of rain and wind had slowly taken away its beauty. What was once a large front yard of lush, green grass was now covered in waist-high yellow weeds—some as tall as the three of us standing there. The winding street turned into a dead end as it became the old Safari House driveway. A long and unruly hedge lined both sides of the driveway, leading visitors up to a cracked walkway. This walkway ran in front of the house and led to steps up to the front porch.

The jog up the hill had made me out of breath. I sucked in air too quickly, and my throat felt like it was on fire. I looked around but didn't see a sign of the kid.

"Where did he go?" I asked.

"He went right in the front door," Scooter answered, pointing toward the front porch of the massive house.

"Well, why did you guys stop chasing him?" I asked.

"Because I'm not going in that scary place," AJ said. "In fact, I'm not even stepping foot on that property. You remember what happened last time we went near that place!"

"I do, but I think we probably just scared ourselves into thinking we saw something that wasn't really there."

"Oh, no way, Ty. That was real. My eyes weren't playing tricks on me; I heard it too!" AJ said, starting to turn back down the hill.

"I agree that it was something—" Scooter began.

"See, Ty, even Scooter agrees," AJ interrupted.

"—but I am not sure I am willing to conclude what that something was. I need more facts," Scooter finished.

AJ whined, "Here is a fact: Nothing is worth entering that house for! We don't know what might be waiting for us in there. I don't care if that kid is our last hope."

"Well, I do care!" I said as I started walking

toward the house. "I want some answers, and that kid is the only way I am going to get any. Scooter, are you coming?"

Scooter began to follow me, which I took as his answer. AJ folded his arms across his chest and exhaled loudly. There was his answer.

As Scooter and I approached the entrance to the driveway, we could see a *For Sale* sign had been uprooted from the overgrown front lawn. It laid uselessly in the tall grass. We continued up the driveway, keeping in the exact middle—what we hoped was a safe distance from the scary-looking hedges on each side. As we walked up the stairs and onto the porch, we could see one of the front windows had been partially broken from what I would guess was a neighborhood kid with a slingshot and decent aim.

Suddenly, there was a loud shrieking from somewhere behind us. It sounded like a bird was dying and wanted everyone to know. I turned to see AJ sprinting up the driveway toward us. Apparently, he decided it was less scary to be with us than standing out in the street with only a dying bird to keep him company.

When we were gathered on the front porch, AJ went to open the front door, but as he reached for the doorknob, the door opened a few inches on its own. AJ freaked out and immediately jumped to the back of our single-file line again.

Now I was in the lead. As I pushed on the door

to open it wider, it made such a loud creaking noise that the hairs on the back of my neck stood straight up. I instinctively held my breath as I stepped inside, as if whatever was in the house couldn't "get me" as long as I didn't breathe.

My eyes slowly adjusted to the lack of daylight inside. I could see that we were in a large entryway. Cobwebs were hanging from everywhere, but luckily none were low enough to run into, because that would have done me in. There is nothing worse than a cobweb in the face! The entryway floor was made of hardwood, and it was surprisingly clean. Straight ahead was a large, carpeted staircase with a decorative wood railing. The dark carpet matched the deep red wallpaper that lined the walls. Several fancy gold frames containing portraits of people and beautiful buildings hung on the walls of the entryway. To our left were a few doors, which were partially open to reveal what looked like a bathroom, study, and guest room. To our right was a carpeted room filled with dining room furniture that had been covered with clear plastic sheets. With the light streaming in from the windows and reflecting off the plastic, the room looked to be full of little ghosts from some ancient video game. Dust was everywhere, and I knew it was just a matter of time before my allergies went into panic mode. As we walked through the dining room, we looked for any sign that the kid had been there.

We quickly moved on to the attached kitchen. We

opened several of the cupboards that looked like they could be potential spots for the kid to hide. Empty. We then circled back to the entryway via a hallway next to the stairs. From there, we went into the rooms on the other side of the entryway. In each room, we looked for any hiding places or any sign the kid had been there. No luck.

"Where did he go?" AJ wondered aloud.

I motioned toward the stairs. Scooter walked over to the bottom of the stairs and shouted toward the second floor, "Hey, come down here! We just want to ask you a couple questions. Then we will leave you alone!"

As he finished yelling, we could hear a small crash coming from upstairs, as if somebody had knocked something over. We waited for a second, but there was no more noise.

"We can wait down here all day if we have to!" I yelled.

AJ shot me a crazed look and shook his head. He was not staying a second longer than he had to. We waited for a few more seconds in silence before Scooter grew restless and began to climb the stairs. AJ whispered under his breath something that ended in "crazy fool" and followed him. I followed a few stairs behind.

We froze at the top of the stairs and listened for any more noises. I could hear a faint *tap-tap-tap* coming from my left. I turned to see a closed doorway at the end of the hall. I tapped AJ on the shoulder and pointed toward the door. AJ now took the lead and quietly tip-toed toward the door. We now could all hear a shuffling sound coming from behind the door. We reached the door, and AJ grabbed the doorknob. The door was designed to swing toward us, so AJ motioned us back a few feet. He looked back at us, mouthed the words "one, two, three," and then flung open the door.

We looked into the small bathroom and froze in fright. Standing on the lid to the toilet was the biggest tiger I had ever seen! It was caught by surprise by the door opening so quickly. The tiger turned its body on the toilet lid in order to face us. It snarled, showing its huge, yellow teeth. The tiger bent his legs and gripped the toilet bowl with his front paws. It was about to pounce!

CHAPTER 1
The Legend of the Old Safari House

So how did we end up in this mess in the first place? Well, this all started about a week ago on a backpacking trip to Flapjack Lakes. My dad, who is in the Navy, had just returned after being on a submarine for the past few months. I was so excited to finally get to spend some time with him now that he was home. He wanted the same thing, and getting some fresh air and elbow room would be an added bonus. Dad and I go hiking often. About half of the time, we go by ourselves, and the other half, we go with my two best friends, AJ and Scooter. Although I had a lot of catching up to do with dear old Dad, this was one of those times that I requested my friends come with us. We had a lot to discuss!

Near the end of our seventh-grade school year, the three of us had formed our own detective agency called the Enigma Squad. We make a pretty good team. Although Scooter is the smallest, he is sort of the leader—mainly because he is super smart. He is always inventing cool gadgets to help us solve our cases (and sometimes to get us out of trouble). If Scooter is the brains of our operation, then AJ would be the muscle. He is so athletic. He's fast and strong, which always seems to come in handy. And I guess you could call me the mouth. My job is to do all the talking. If we have a run-in with an adult, I am the one to talk our way out of it. That is, if AJ doesn't stick his foot in his mouth first. For three junior-highers, we hadn't done too badly so far. We were already becoming pretty well known in our hometown of Silverdale, Washington.

I wanted to bring AJ and Scooter along because I figured with all the hiking we were going to be doing, we would have plenty of time to discuss things—and we had a lot to talk about! I had been grounded to my room since we solved *The Case of the Bike in the Birdcage,* and I felt like there were unanswered questions involving the case.

So Dad and I spent the first part of the hike catching up on life at home while he had been away. Scooter and AJ set a fast pace and stayed a good distance ahead of us. After about an hour, my dad told me to go be with my friends, and so I did.

The three of us spent the rest of the hike up to our campsite talking about our last case. I won't get into the details (it's probably best if you just read the case file for yourself), but the one thing I just had to discuss was what I had discovered while documenting the case afterward. I had found a clue about our new "person of interest," A.F. (the only name we had to go on). I was still puzzled as to how much involvement this A.F. had with our last case, and I was hoping AJ and Scooter might help me think things through. They were not much help.

We talked in circles about A.F. for at least a half hour, and we couldn't agree on anything. I mean, what did we really know about him? Almost nothing. In the end, we decided to stop worrying about A.F. for the time being. Boy, would that decision come back to haunt us!

We found a nice spot near the lake to set up camp. By the time we got there, we were starving, but unfortunately, all the equipment for cooking dinner was in my dad's backpack. Who knew how far behind he was! The three of us decided instead to set up the tents that we had carried in our packs: a two-man tent for my dad to sleep in alone and a three-man tent for the three of us boys to squeeze into. It seems that most tents fit half as many people inside as they claim to.

We were putting the rain cover on the last tent as my dad dragged himself into camp. He looked pretty tired, but when he saw the tents already set up, he began to smile. Thirty minutes later, we were sitting around a blazing fire, enjoying some mac and cheese mixed with canned tuna. That might not sound very good to you, but don't knock it until you have tried it. Besides, even if tuna is not your favorite, after hiking all day, anything tastes good. I remember once after a big hike, our guide served us chili with huge chunks of onion in it. I cannot stand onions, but I wolfed down that whole bowl of chili and was begging for seconds.

Anyway, after dinner we cleaned up and then sat around the fire, and AJ began to re-tell every scary story he had ever heard. Frankly, none of them was very scary. I know some pretty good stories myself, but AJ and Scooter have already heard them on some of our previous trips. Unlike AJ, I try not to tell the same stories over and over.

Finally, Scooter spoke up, "So, Mr. Pate, do you know any scary stories?"

Dad looked up from the little stick he had been whittling with his favorite pocketknife. "Oh, sure, I know plenty of stories." With a small grin, he turned his attention back to his wood carving.

AJ shot me a look that said, "Say something!"

So I did: "Well, Dad, can you share one with us?"

"Oh, I am sure I *can*. I am quite capable of telling a good story." He said this without looking up. My dad had said something similar many times before. It was his *subtle* way of correcting my grammar—people seemed to be correcting me a lot lately, and it was starting to get on my nerves.

"Sorry, *will* you tell us a scary story?"

My dad perked right up, "Sure!" He then set his stick and pocketknife down and leaned forward so his face was aglow in the campfire's light.

"Tell us the scariest one you know," AJ dared.

"Scariest one, huh? Well, this one is probably the scariest—mostly because it's true!"

The three of us skeptics groaned out loud.

"You haven't even heard the story yet! You might think differently once I finish."

"I highly doubt that," muttered the analytical Scooter.

"Well, like I said, this story is scary because it is actually a true story, but also because it takes place so close to home."

Okay, now I knew which story he was going to tell. I had heard it before on a previous father–son trip. I wondered if he would be able to tell this story the same way he had the last time.

My dad leaned toward the fire even more and lowered his voice almost to a whisper, forcing us to lean in as well in order to hear him better.

"So this true story takes place in our little town of Silverdale about sixty years ago. There was this very rich man named Henry Webb. He had a very wealthy family, who were in the furniture business in New York. He decided to move out to our small town in Washington in order to get away from the chaos of New York City and to get away from his relatives, who wanted him to take over the family furniture business. Henry did not want to work in that business. In fact, he did not want to have to work at all. So he took his small share of the family money and moved out West.

"Henry bought a piece of land at the top of Hidden Place and built a fairly large house there. It was huge for just one person, but not nearly as huge as the mansion he had lived in before. He could not afford to live as luxuriously as he had back in New York, when his family was paying for everything."

Scooter and AJ looked at each other. I know exactly what they were thinking. Hidden Place is a road fairly close to the neighborhood we all live in. It is a road that twists and turns up a steep hill, and at the top is a large, old house. You can actually see the house from the bottom of the hill because it rises above the rooftops of the other houses farther down the hill. We passed by Hidden Place every time we went into town from our house. If my dad was making this story up, he was doing a good job of including enough real-life facts to make it sound real!

My dad saw us looking at each other, "So you know which house I'm talking about? That's good, because that's what this story is all about, as you will see.

"Well, after Henry Webb built his house, a friend of his took him hunting for the first time in his life. He had never seen much wildlife while living in New York City, and so he really enjoyed the experience. He wanted to go again and again. Pretty soon he was spending every chance he got hunting anything and everything he could. Henry got bored very easily, though, so he kept hunting bigger and bigger animals in order to challenge himself. First it was fox and coyote. Then deer and elk. Pretty soon he was taking trips to Alaska to hunt moose and bear. He even took a trip to Wyoming to hunt the mighty buffalo.

"Henry Webb started to become famous because of some of his hunting adventures, and soon people began paying him to take them hunting and be their guide. Henry realized he could make money as a hunting guide, and he wouldn't have to 'work' another day in his life. He started taking people all over the Northwest to hunt. Washington, Oregon, Idaho, even Alaska. The farther he took them, the more money he could charge them for the travel expenses. Then he got really bold and started to take these people to other continents. Eventually, he took some folks to Africa, and that is where he really began enjoying himself. He hunted for animals you or I wouldn't want to see in person except at a zoo: lions, tigers, elephants, crocodiles, and other extremely dangerous animals.

"After a few years of traveling back and forth to Africa, he had built himself an incredible reputation because of his expeditions. And now he had tons of money because he could charge so much money to take rich people on these trips to Africa. But as I said before, Henry was a man who got bored very easily, and he began to get bored of these hunting trips too. So he decided to get even more daring: he would try and catch these exotic animals alive! And he actually succeeded! So now every time he went on a safari, he came back with some new exotic animal in a cage, and he put them in different rooms in his house! So that house at the top of Hidden Place became known as the Safari House. People would come and pay Henry Webb, and he would let them into his house to see all his different animals from Africa. It was better than a zoo!"

"That's totally illegal!" AJ spoke up. It is scary how much AJ seems to know about what is or isn't legal.

"You're right, AJ. Nowadays that would be true," Dad continued, "but 60 years ago, there were a lot fewer laws and even fewer police to enforce what laws there were. Now, here is where it gets interesting—and scary.

"So people think that Henry Webb then went crazy. He eventually stopped letting people see his animals, and then he stopped traveling so that he could spend all his time with his 'babies'—that's what he called his pets. People say he believed he could actually train his animals to be indoor pets. He started letting certain animals out of their cages to roam around the house with him.

"Of course, that was just a rumor. No one had any proof he was crazy enough to actually do it… until one day, when the mailman went up to the front porch to deliver the mail. He noticed the mail had not been picked up for a few days, so he started to wonder if everything were okay with Mr. Webb.

He peeked in the front window. The room was completely trashed! He saw lamps broken, furniture knocked over, and the couch torn to shreds. Then, while the mailman was staring at all this through the window, a lion walked around the corner from the kitchen. It went right up to the window and roared right in the mailman's face!

"The police were notified, of course, and they tried to call the Safari House phone. But no one answered. Everyone was too scared of the lion to enter the house, so they eventually just opened the front door. When the lion came out of the house, they shot it. Then when they went inside, they found what they had feared: Henry Webb had been killed by the lion. And it looked like he had indeed let the lion out of its cage on purpose. The police found a whole bunch of other animals still in their cages, but since no one in the small town knew how to take care of the exotic animals—and probably because they were scared of what they didn't know—they had all the animals put to sleep."

"That's horrible!" AJ jumped in.

"And not scary," Scooter added.

"Well, I was just getting to the scary part," my dad continued. "Now, they say the old Safari House is haunted by Henry Webb and all the animals that were once in the house. From the day the police took the cages out of that house, the neighbors claimed they could see all sorts of animals roaming around the neighborhood: lions, gorillas, crocodiles, and all sorts of animals you wouldn't normally find in Washington.

"The reason it still sits empty at the top of Hidden Place is because no one is brave enough to stay in it very long. Over the years, three different people have bought that house and moved in. Two families moved back out right away because they couldn't stand all the animal noises they heard while they were trying to sleep. They swore they saw safari animals roaming the halls at night. The third family moved in about twenty years ago and was never heard from again. They say all of their stuff is still in the house, gathering dust even to this day.

"Even now the neighbors say at night you might see an exotic animal wander through the yard. Some nights you can even hear a lion roar or a monkey chattering." Dad leaned in closer and lowered his voice more and more: "And every great while… you can hear… what sounds like… a human scream. Augh!" Dad screamed in fright, making all three of us jump—even though I knew it was coming. And then he calmly leaned back away from the fire.

"Great story," Scooter complimented.

"Oh, it's not a story," Dad said with a wink. "It's more of a warning. Don't go near the old Safari House. You might get eaten!"

"I knew it! It's true," AJ blurted out. "Lately I keep hearing these weird noises outside my window late at night. I could never figure out what they were, but now I know! It's a bunch of monkeys trying to get in my window from the outside!"

"Boy, AJ, if you could just use that imagination for something more productive," I mocked.

"It's not his imagination. Like I said before, this is a true story." My dad was doing a good job of keeping a straight face. "In fact, you can ask any of our neighbors or anyone else who has been around Silverdale for a while, they will all tell you the same thing that I just did. Go ahead, ask them about the origins of the old Safari House, or ask them who Henry Webb is."

"You mean *was,* Dad." I tried to correct him.

"No, I mean *is,* Tyler. Henry Webb is still very much around. At least his ghost is."

Scooter was not buying it, and it was also past his bedtime. "Thanks, Mr. Pate, but that's enough scary stories for me. True or imaginary. Good night, everyone." He stood up and walked over to our tent only a few feet away.

I stood and followed him. "Good night, Dad. I love you."

My dad stood. "Love you too, Son."

AJ stood, took a step toward my dad, and half-whispered, "I believe you." He then turned to join Scooter and me. With our backs to the campfire, we heard the loud hiss as dad poured a bucket of water on the fire in order to douse it. Unfortunately, the flames now burning in AJ's imagination would be much harder to put out.

CHAPTER 2
Monkey Business

I thought we had heard the last of that story. but when we woke up the next morning, it was clear I was wrong. We went fishing most of the morning, but AJ did his best to take the fun out of it.

About every five minutes, he would ask something like, "Do you really think a lion could survive living in Washington? Do you think they can stand all the rain? Do you think an alligator or crocodile could live inside a house?" Clearly, my dad's scary story was on his mind.

Although Scooter and I were highly annoyed with AJ, the fish didn't seem to care. They were biting pretty well. We ended up catching three trout that were keepers and a couple we had to throw back in because they were too small.

Finally, the weather got hotter around lunchtime, and we went swimming. We were pretty high up in the mountains, and therefore the lake was practically freezing. The key to swimming in a lake that cold is to jump in, rather than try slowly wading in. If you try wading in, the second the water gets above your knees, your brain sends a message to the rest of your body demanding that you don't move another inch. Instead, you have to just dive in and cause your whole body to go into shock at the same time! Sticking my head underwater gave me the worst headache, but it was still better than having to listen to AJ's constant questions. Later that afternoon we built a huge fort out of fallen logs. The task seemed to take up enough of AJ's attention that we thought he might have forgotten about the old Safari House and all the animals. But we were wrong.

After preparing, eating, and then cleaning up after dinner, it was starting to get dark. The tall evergreens were casting long shadows over the campsite.

AJ now started to ask, "Did you hear that? What was that? Did something just move over there?"

I tried to tell AJ that even if the legend of the Safari House was real, the animals would not have traveled a hundred miles to our camping spot just to scare him. He was not convinced.

I have to admit, the temptation was too much to resist. The rest of the night, I started to ask every so often, "Did you guys hear that? Do you see what I see over there in the shadows?"

Scooter caught on and joined my little game, "Oh yeah, I think I hear it too!"

AJ freaked out a little more every time we said

something—it was hilarious. That night, I am not sure that he slept at all!

The next morning we continued to razz him as we ate breakfast and broke down camp. The daylight made him a little less chicken, and he adopted a new strategy of simply ignoring us. In fact, he stayed a good ways ahead of us the entire hike back. When we got to the car, Scooter knew it would be an unbearable car ride home if AJ did not talk to us.

"Listen, Aidge, we are sorry. We were just giving you a hard time."

"Yeah, sorry, AJ," I added.

"You guys don't understand! To you this is still a joke, but I am serious. I've seen things, heard things," he said emphatically.

"Okay, okay, we believe you," I said, trying hard not to laugh or even smile. "Let's just forget about it for now, okay?"

"Fine!" AJ said with finality. And sure enough, the entire car ride home was filled with discussion about the Seattle Mariners, and school in the fall, and other random stuff, but not a mention of haunted houses or exotic animals.

After driving AJ and Scooter to their houses, just down the street, my dad and I finally pulled into our driveway. It had been a fun trip but also exhausting. All I wanted to do was dump my backpack just inside the door of the garage, head upstairs, and plop my tired body on my bed for an emergency nap. In fact, I started to do that, but as I dropped my backpack and started to head into the house, my dad stopped me.

"And where do you think you're going?" he asked without even looking in my direction. He had opened his pack and was already putting some of the camping gear onto its proper shelves along the back wall of the garage.

"Uh, I was going to go take a nap. I am soooooo tired." I moaned to emphasize how tired I was. "I'll unpack my stuff when I wake up."

"No, you should unpack it now. Otherwise that pack will still be sitting there three weeks from now."

"But, Dad, I am exhausted."

"Excuse me? Did you somehow hike more than I did? I'm pretty sure you and I went up and down the same mountain."

"Yeah, but you're an adult. And I'm just a kid." I am not sure I knew what the point of my argument was anymore.

My dad stopped what he was doing and stared at me. "Tyler..." It was only one word, but I had heard it said in that tone many times before. I knew the argument was over.

"Yes, sir." I brought my backpack over next to his to begin putting my stuff away.

His tense face relaxed, and with a smile and a nod he said, "Thank you" and reached up and fussed with my dirty hair.

It did not take long to put things away, and I was then free to go take as long a nap as I wanted. I probably should have taken a shower first, but instead I just fell onto my bed with all of my clothes still on. It felt so good I just stayed there with my feet hanging off the end of my bed. I wondered if I could actually fall asleep in that position. I thought about it for about fifteen seconds before I was gone.

When I woke up it was four hours later, and it was fairly dark in my room. My mother had called me for dinner at six, but when I surprisingly did not show up, she came upstairs to find me fast asleep. She decided not to wake me, but instead she just pulled my shoes off my feet and turned off the bedroom light.

Now I don't know about you, but I find it very disorienting to go to sleep when it is light out and wake up in the dark. I sat up in bed and tried to remember where I was or how I had gotten there. I had no clue what time it was, but my stomach started growling at me. That clued me in that my dinner was long overdue.

I went downstairs and found my sister, Tamara, laying on the couch, watching one of her favorite TV shows—some reality game show involving wedding cakes. She watched that show every night of the summer at 9 p.m., so I knew the time must be sometime after 9. You know you might be watching too much TV when you can tell time based on what show is on.

I went into the kitchen and found a bag of chips from the cupboard and some salsa from the fridge. I plopped myself down in the chair next to the couch my sister was on and began eating my "dinner." I wasn't really interested in a show about making cakes, but I was still trying to wake up fully. And I also knew the *crunch-crunch* of the chips would drive Tamara bonkers.

Sure enough, right on cue, she sat up on the couch and whined, "Tyler! Do you have to eat those in here? I am watching my show!"

"Then watch it; don't let me stop you!" I shot back.

"But I can't hear anything besides your crunching!"

"Why do you need to hear anyway?" I argued. "Not only do you want to see someone make a boring cake, you want to hear them talk about it too?"

"Yes! Now leave!" she yelled in frustration.

I am not sure where my parents were at the moment, but I knew if Tamara got any louder, they would probably hear it and come to her rescue—and that would spell trouble for me. I had had my moment of enjoyment at my sister's expense, and I was ready to leave her alone anyway.

As I stood up to head back to the kitchen, I heard a familiar knock on the living room window: *bump-bah-duh-duh-bump-bump-bump*. It was the official knock of the Enigma Squad. That meant either Scooter or AJ was outside the window in the front yard. I told Tamara I would be right back, slipped on a pair of shoes that were sitting by the front door, and went out onto my front steps.

When I got outside, an anxious AJ was hopping up and down, waiting to see me. I smiled, "Hi, AJ, do you need to borrow our bathroom or something?"

"Ha ha, very funny, Ty. Listen, this is for real! I saw them!"

"Saw who?" I asked confused.

"The monkeys!" His eyes were as big as golf balls as he retold his story. "I was up in my room, and I heard that same scratching noise outside my window. I quickly ran over to the window, and I saw the monkeys jump over the fence into the neighbor's yard!"

"Monkeys," I said with a frown. "You saw monkeys outside your window?"

"Yes, I saw them. I swear!"

"Dude, you gotta stop with this, AJ. It's just a story! My dad made it up! The whole Safari House thing was just to scare us."

"I know what I saw, Ty!"

It was clear I was not going to be able to convince AJ he was just seeing things—at least not by myself. "Have you told Scooter this yet?"

"No, I came here first. I saw you watching TV through the window; that's why I knocked."

"Okay, let's go talk to Scooter." I turned to go back in the front door. "Wait here a sec."

I opened the front door to find Tamara still laying on the couch watching her cake show. "Tell Mom and Dad I will be back in about fifteen minutes."

"They won't be back till late; they went to watch a movie," she said without even looking away from the TV.

"Even better," I said. "See ya."

She responded without saying a word, just a half-hearted wave as I went back out the front door.

CHAPTER 3

The Search for Henry Webb

AJ and I walked in the middle of the street toward Scooter's house. AJ and I lived on the same street with a house in between us, while Scooter lived just a few houses away, on a connecting street. When we got to Scooter's house, we could see all the lights were off downstairs, but several of the bedroom lights were on upstairs, including Scooter's bedroom.

"It looks like we will have to make a call to Triple-A, huh?" I asked.

"Yup," AJ agreed.

Triple-A is the name Scooter came up with for one of his many inventions. You see, our parents were starting to get annoyed at all the late-evening phone calls we were making to each other. Although it was summer and we boys could sleep in if we wanted, most of our parents still had to get up early to go to work. They did not appreciate the phone ringing after dark and waking them from their precious sleep. So Scoot came up with his "Alternate Alert Apparatus," or AAA. He like to joke and say, "making a call to Triple-A." The name was more complicated than the actual device. Basically, Scooter took a piece of fishing line and tied it to a piece of metal. Then he threaded the fishing line through the bottom of a small tin can, and then he ran the fishing line out of his window and down the side of his house to the first floor.

AJ went over to the side of the house below Scooter's window and fumbled around in the dark until he found the fishing line hanging down. He pulled on the string a couple times. The metal attached to the other end of the string rattled around inside the can in Scooter's room. In the quiet of the evening, we could actually hear the rattling even though we were outside the house.

Scooter's face appeared immediately in the window. He cracked his window open enough to talk to us. "What's up?" he asked.

"HQ," I said.

"Okay," he said as he shut the window and disappeared from view.

HQ refers to the Enigma Squad's secret headquarters. When we first started our detective agency, we found a bomb shelter buried in Scooter's backyard that had been long since forgotten by just about everyone. The only entrance to the shelter is a metal plate buried underneath a heaping mound of blackberries. Getting to that metal plate underneath the blackberries does have a few options, though.

We built or expanded three different tunnels through the berry bushes to the plate. The Straight-a-Way is a tunnel that runs back along the property line between Scooter's yard and the yard of his neighbor. The Straight-a-Way ends at a secret door made of blackberry vines, deep in the woods behind Scooter's house. The Right Hook veers off to the right from the Straight-a-Way. It too ends at a secret door that is much closer to Scooter's backyard. The third and final tunnel goes directly west from the plate and dead-ends at the Langsworths' (Scoot's neighbors) wood fence. We have not had time to figure out how to make a door in the fence yet, so that tunnel is not being used yet. When we do figure it out, it will be called the Emergency Exit because it will be the fastest way into or out of HQ, but it will open right into the Langsworths' yard.

Since it was dark and there was no chance of being seen, AJ and I decided to take the Right Hook. We walked across Scooter's backyard, and when we had walked into the woods a few steps, AJ turned and walked right up to the tall, thick blackberry bushes that ran alongside the yard. AJ slowly reached into the prickly bushes and moved a stick. Then as he pulled his hand back, an entire mass of blackberry branches moved with it. This was the camouflage door of the entrance. Behind this wall was the Right Hook tunnel. AJ swung the door out of his way and entered first. I followed behind and reached back to close the door. As I swung the door closed, I heard a "Hold up," and Scooter appeared. I smiled and let him take over the duties of getting the door closed.

The three of us then crouched and hobbled our way down the tunnel toward the metal plate, the entrance to HQ. This ridiculous mode of transportation has now become known as the "squat-walk." Yes, it is as ridiculous-looking as it sounds, but it's the only way to avoid getting scratched to death by blackberry vines.

At the end of the tunnel is the metal plate. AJ lifted it and quickly descended the ladder beneath it. Once all three of us were inside and Scooter had closed the lid above us, I pushed a big button attached to the wall, and the big button began to glow. This button was a dome light, and it was all that was needed to dimly light the entire room. The room wasn't that big, anyway. It wasn't much bigger than a closet—a closet made of cement. And there's nothing in the room, either, except for a ladder on one wall and a large vault door on the opposite wall.

The large door required a key. AJ had one hanging around his neck, attached to a metal chain, and he pulled it out from underneath his T-shirt. We had recently made copies, and now there were five copies in total. Each of the three of us had one that usually hung around our necks. One was hidden in a tree in Scooter's backyard, and one was stashed under Scooter's mattress in his room—just in case we lost the other four!

AJ used his key to unlock the door, and with a heave, he pulled open the thick, metal door.

Inside the shelter we were fully hooked up. There was a futon, a chair, a small table, and even a phone. There was also a sink, a toilet (only for *extreme* emergencies) surrounded by curtains, and—probably our favorite part—a full-sized refrigerator! All these things were in the bomb shelter when we discovered it. How lucky were we! The only major thing we changed after moving in was to bring Scooter's super-duper computer down here, with a desk and chair for it. Although the actual computer was now in HQ, Scooter could somehow still access it from up in his bedroom with a small computer he had up there. It took a little bit of creative wiring, I guess, but Scooter's a genius so I am sure it wasn't hard for him at all.

As usual, AJ headed straight for the fridge, Scooter sat down in his chair in front of his computer, and I plopped down on the futon.

"So, what's up, guys?" Scooter asked.

"AJ says he saw a monkey," I stated matter-of-factly.

"AJ, we have been over this!" Scooter said with some frustration. "It was just a story!"

AJ shook his head, turning away from the fridge, "I know what I saw, Scoot!"

"Whatever, AJ," Scooter said as he rolled his eyes.

AJ turned to me. "Your dad said we could ask around to verify his story. How about we check online? I bet you we'll find something that proves his story."

"Okay then," Scooter agreed, "but if we don't find anything, will you agree to drop this?"

"Deal!" AJ said confidently.

Scooter turned around in his chair to face his computer and began typing. "Okay, so I am just going to enter a few keywords in the search engine here: Silverdale, Safari House, haunted house, and what was that guy's name again?"

"Henry Webb," I immediately answered.

Scooter shot me a surprised look because I had remembered. "Wow, okay."

"My dad has actually told me that story before," I explained.

Scooter chuckled. He figured that was just more proof that the story was made up. He added Henry Webb to the list of keywords and began the search.

The computer spit out results in less than a second. There were several newspaper articles from the last twenty years. Lots of stories listed people who claimed they had seen the animals late at night, and one story told all about the Safari House and how people used to come from Seattle just to see a tiger in person. It even had a black-and-white photo of Henry Webb himself, holding a rifle and wearing a safari helmet.

"Ha," AJ said triumphantly. "I knew it was a true story!"

"Hold on," Scooter argued. "We are not saying that Henry Webb did not exist. We are just telling you that you are imagining animals that are not there."

"I know what I saw!" said AJ.

"AJ, those animals from the Safari House would have to be over sixty years old now!"

"But you heard Mr. Pate: these are ghost animals."

"There is no such thing as a ghost," Scooter argued. "It's illogical!"

"You're wrong," AJ said and then pointed at the computer screen. "And it looks like there are plenty of people out there who agree with me." AJ grabbed an apple off the counter and took a bite while staring at us. Apparently, this was his way of telling us the conversation was over.

Scooter wasn't finished, though. "How about this: tomorrow we go up to the Safari House and prove once and for all who is right."

"But the animals only come out at night!" AJ said. Apparently, he had this all thought out.

"Okay, fine," Scooter conceded. "We will go up during the day and check things out. Then we will find a good place to camp out and go back at night. Will that satisfy you?"

"Fine," AJ said.

"Fine," Scooter said.

"Fine," I jumped in. "Let's meet at my house at 10 tomorrow morning."

CHAPTER 4

Settling the Debate on Hidden Place

The next day when I stepped out of my front door, both AJ and Scooter were already there with their bikes, and they had picked up right where they had left off over the existence of ghosts.

I interrupted, "So you guys ready? Let's go find a ghost!"

Scooter shot me a dirty look.

"Or not," I laughed uncomfortably.

The bike ride to Hidden Place was very short. When we got to the bottom of the hill, we all looked up toward the top and the old Safari House. Its weathered roof rose above the other roofs of the houses down below. It was almost mocking us, taunting us to come up and face the Safari House if we dared.

Scooter took this chance to get one more dig in. "Okay, AJ. Last chance to turn around before we make you look bad."

AJ laughed him off and began pedaling his bike up the steep, winding hill. Scooter and I tried to follow him. The hill was so steep that we only lasted a few feet before we all decided to hop off our bikes and walk them the rest of the way up. We could have ditched our bikes at the bottom of the hill, but then we would miss the awesome chance to fly back down the hill later.

When we finally turned the last corner, we could see the old Safari House looming in front of us. Unlike all the neighbors below with their nicely cut lawns, the entire Safari House property had long, yellow grass, which would come up to our waists or higher—that is if we were actually crazy enough to walk through it. I didn't believe in animal ghosts, but that didn't stop me from imagining a lion sneaking through the tall grass, stalking us like prey. To avoid the tall grass, we decided not to take a shortcut across the yard. Instead, we would take the longer way, using the driveway, which had its own share of grass growing from the cracks in the cement.

The only way to tell where the road ended and the Safari House driveway began was the two hedges that ran the length of the driveway on both sides. I am sure that once upon a time the bushes had been well-trimmed and beautiful, but years of neglect had turned them into eyesores. At the entrance to the driveway, we all stopped, set our bikes down, and looked at the massive house. The house had been green long ago, but many, many years of direct sunlight on top of the hill had faded the paint to a point that the house almost looked a dirty yellow. Many of the wood shingles from the roof had cracked, and a few had fallen helplessly to the broken walkway below. The roof over the large front porch was sagging, and even in the bright sun, the shadows made it too dark to see much near the front door.

"Well, here we go," Scooter said and took the first step forward.

AJ made an audible *gulp* sound and followed.

I was about to bring up the rear when we suddenly heard a loud hissing noise. Everybody froze in their tracks. The sound was coming from the overgrown hedge to our right. The hissing seemed to be getting louder.

"S-s-s-snake," AJ stuttered. "I hate snakes!"

"I have never heard of a snake that hissed that loudly before," Scooter argued.

We slowly started to back down the driveway towards our bikes. I kept my eye on the bushes. They were at least ten feet away, and in my mind if a snake appeared, I had a good ten-foot head start on getting away. Snakes can't move that fast, right? Suddenly, I saw something large move near the base of the bushes. Someone yelled, "Alligator!" and someone else yelled, "Crocodile!" at practically the same time. Then I heard AJ scream something unintelligible. He zipped past me and grabbed his bike.

"Run!" Scooter screamed. He too had his bike before I knew what was happening.

I didn't know what it was. At the moment, I didn't care. I turned and bolted for my bike. We three flew down the winding hill as fast as we could.

After racing down the hill, we kept on pedaling all the way to AJ's house. We had not agreed to go to AJ's house, but since he never stopped pedaling until he got there (and he was so much faster than Scooter and me), we didn't really have a choice but to follow.

When we got to AJ's driveway and could finally catch our breath, I blurted out, "Wha-Wha-What was that?"

"I don't know. I need something to eat before I can think," AJ said, surprisingly out of breath.

Scooter and I weren't going to argue with that, so we all went inside to find some lunch. Normally, AJ's house has really good food, but today we had to settle for ham sandwiches and potato chips. I think we were all a little too preoccupied to complain about the menu.

As I finished my sandwich, I commented, "Wow! I am still shaking from seeing that alligator."

"Crocodile," Scooter corrected.

"I don't even know the difference," AJ said with a mouth full of potato chips.

"Crocodiles have pointy, V-shaped snouts, while alligators have rounded, U-shaped ones. Crocodiles are also usually lighter in color, and their fourth pair of bottom teeth sticks up outside their mouths," Scooter announced. It figures he would know that.

"So, wait… which one did we just run into?" I asked. "I didn't exactly stick around to get a good look at it."

"Me neither! I saw Baby Godzilla and ran!" AJ exclaimed.

Scooter answered, "I think it was a crocodile, but neither are really native to this area. Alligators can be found mainly in Florida and other places in the Southeast United States. Some species of crocodiles can be found all over the world, but the majority are found in exotic places like—"

"Africa?" AJ jumped in to finish his sentence. "See? The legend is real! I can't believe we just saw a ghost crocodile!"

I began to laugh at AJ's absurd statement. I looked over at Scooter, but he wasn't laughing. Instead, he had his thinking face on. It's this sort of half-smile, half-frown thing he does when he is working out some problem in his head.

"What do you think, Scoot?" I asked, still trying to decide what I really thought.

"It defies logic to be sure," Scooter said, scratching the top of his head. "I find it hard to believe it was a ghost, but I don't really have a better explanation."

AJ stood up from the table and raised both his fists in the air like a champion of a boxing fight. "I was right, and poor little Scooter was wrong!"

"Yeah, you had better mark this date on your calendar. This is a once-in-a-lifetime event," Scooter grumbled and then took a bite of his sandwich.

AJ took a few victory laps around the table and then sat back down. "So what do we do now?"

"What do you mean 'what do we do now?' You were right. What more do you want?" Scooter sounded pretty annoyed.

"Well, we have to figure out what they want," AJ said with conviction.

"What who wants?" I asked.

"The ghost animals! Don't most ghosts have unfinished business? That's why they haunt people. We need to figure out what the ghosts want."

"Wow, AJ, you do watch way too much TV!" Now even I was annoyed.

"AJ, I might admit you were right for once, but there is no way I am going to help you with that stupid idea!" Scooter argued.

"Fine, I don't need your help. I will just use The Network," AJ said. The Network was a group of fans of the Enigma Squad that we would sometimes use to help us solve cases. If we were looking for something or someone, we could send out a request to The Network, who would then make the same request to all their friends, who would make the same request to *their* friends, and on and on. One mass email to The Network asking for any sightings of exotic animals could result in hundreds of people looking on our behalf.

AJ continued his thought, "I am sure there are people out there who have seen things and heard things, who want answers just like me."

"Knock yourself out," Scooter said.

"Great! Let's go!" AJ said as he stood up and put his lunch plate in the sink.

"Go where?" Scooter said without moving an inch.

"Down to HQ, so we can send a message to The Network."

"I am not going anywhere. You are on your own. Just try not to blow up my computer while you are down there," Scooter replied.

"Fine!" AJ huffed as he headed toward the front door. Then he stopped and turned around. "Actually, you can't stay here. Get out of my house."

"You're kicking us out?" I asked, surprised. After all, we practically lived at each other's houses.

"Yup. If you guys are going to be jerks and not help me, then you can be jerks somewhere else!"

"Fine." Scooter stood abruptly and tossed his plate in the sink, even though it still had some food on it. "Ty, can we go hang out at your place?"

"Uh, sure, yeah, I guess," I said as I stuffed the last of my sandwich in my mouth.

Scooter and I marched past an angry AJ, who didn't say a word but just held the front door open and bit his lower lip.

Scooter and I decided to spend the afternoon cooling down and playing some chess. I knew Scooter would beat me every time, but I didn't really care. I was just going through the motions anyway. I was too busy thinking about AJ. He was not very computer-savvy, so I was very curious to know if he was able to get a message off to The Network or not.

I lost track of how many times Scooter beat me before my mom came into the kitchen, where we were playing. She announced we were headed over to Seattle to visit Great-aunt Fran, who had just had her hip replaced. My mom said it was time for Scooter to go home. We cleaned up the chess pieces, and I told Scooter I would catch up with him the next day.

CHAPTER 5
Help Wanted

We did not get home until very late from our trip to see my great-aunt, and so I slept in rather late the next morning. When I woke, I was excited to smell bacon coming from downstairs. I stumbled down the stairs and into the kitchen to get my share. I was disappointed to find that my mom was actually washing the morning dishes. I had missed breakfast entirely! While I stood there with a puzzled look on my face, my dad walked in from the garage with a sweaty forehead. He had been "tinkering in the garage" for much of the morning.

"Well, good morning, sleepy-head!" he said a little too loudly for my taste. "Glad to see you decided to join us." He opened the fridge and pulled out a bottled water.

"I guess I missed out on the bacon, huh?" I mumbled.

"You should have," my mother said, "but I actually saved you a plate of food. It is sitting in the microwave."

I reached over and pulled open the microwave door. Inside was a plate of French toast, eggs, and of course, bacon! An involuntary smile snuck onto my face. "Thanks, Mom." I pushed the *+30 Seconds* button and went to fetch a fork.

"Oh, and Scooter called about a half hour ago and said when you finally wake up, you should meet him in his backyard."

"Great!" I said and then sat to wolf down my meal.

After breakfast I quickly got changed and headed down the street to Scooter's house. I assumed when he said his backyard, he was referring to HQ, which was located more or less in his backyard. I was also curious what he had called about. I guess that AJ must have actually sent out a message correctly and that this morning we were going to be analyzing any responses we got back.

When I entered HQ, I was greeted by an excited AJ. "Guess what, Ty? We got ourselves a job!"

Scooter could see that I was confused. "We got an email this morning from a girl who wants to hire us. Here." He handed me a printout of the email. Here is what is said:

Dear Enigma Squad,

I need your help, and I am hoping you will assist me because the police won't. A couple days ago, I was celebrating my birthday at my grandma's house. I invited a few of my high-school friends over, including Jerry, who I thought was my best friend. During the party, my friend Jerry had gone upstairs to use the bathroom. Then, just a few minutes later, he abruptly had to go "take care of something" and left the party early. Later my grandma's ruby ring was discovered to be missing from her upstairs bedroom. My grandma is so upset about the whole thing. I know it was stupid Jerry that took the ring because he is the only one who ever went upstairs during the party. When I confronted him about it later, he denied everything, and now he is avoiding speaking to me!

I went to the police, but they can't do anything unless I can prove that Jerry has the ring. So I want to hire you guys to follow Jerry and catch him with the ring. I bet you anything he is going to try and sell it. Jerk! Anyway, then I will have proof and can turn Jerry over to the police. Please let me know if you will take the job, and I can let you know where you might be able to find Jerry. I know his schedule pretty well. (Like I said, we used to be best friends before he turned into a two-faced liar.)

Sincerely,

Angela Fitzpatrick

"Dude, that's messed up," I said as I handed the email back to Scooter.

"That's kind of what I thought," Scooter agreed.

"This girl sounds like she has some anger issues!" I joked.

"That's also what I thought," Scooter chuckled.

"So let's make sure we don't do anything to tick her off!" I added. "We are taking this case, right?"

"All in favor say 'Aye,'" AJ chimed in.

"Aye!" all three of us said in unison.

"Okay, I will shoot her an email telling her we will help her," Scooter said as he began pecking away at his keyboard.

After Scooter finished his email, AJ had a little show-and-tell for us. Apparently, his mom had bought him a used cell phone the night before. After our last case, his mom didn't want us to ever be in a place where we couldn't make a call for help.

When he flipped the silver phone open, the Seattle Mariners logo was pictured in the background. The phone was a few years old, but it did have a couple games for when you had some time to kill, including solitaire. Unfortunately, he was only supposed to use it during emergencies.

In the middle of all this, Scooter heard a chime on his computer alerting him of an incoming email. He clicked on it to discover it was from Angela. Wow, that was fast! It had only been about five minutes since Scooter had sent his email taking the case.

It was clear Angela was anxious for us to get

started, mostly because she knew exactly where Jerry would be for the next two hours. Apparently every day Jerry would go to the YMCA from 10 till noon. She thought the best chance to pick up on Jerry's trail was to catch him at the Y. He rode a green bike with white flames, and we would be able to find him that way. Scooter sent a quick email in reply to tell her thanks for the tip.

"It sounds like we have about two hours to get down there and set up," Scooter said as he stood up from the computer. "Let's get packed and ready to go."

"Okay, what should we bring? We have no clue how long it could take to follow him," AJ said.

"You two just go get your bikes and a backpack with a couple of waters each," Scooter instructed. "We probably will be doing a lot of bike riding. I will take care of the rest."

"Meet up at my house?" I asked.

"Sure, sounds good," Scooter agreed. "Give me about fifteen minutes to pack up a couple of gadgets." Scooter was always looking for a chance to use some of his many inventions.

Ten minutes later, AJ and I were sitting on our bikes in my driveway, waiting in anticipation for Scooter to show up. Fortunately, we did not have to wait that long. A couple minutes later, Scooter came pedaling down the street with a heavily loaded backpack. With Scooter being fairly small, the backpack almost seemed bigger than he was!

As he huffed and puffed his way to my driveway, I just had to ask, "So Scooter, what *didn't* you bring?"

AJ and I both laughed at our tired friend.

"I cannot be sure of the circumstances we might encounter during our surveillance," Scooter said as he opened his backpack. He pulled out a couple walkie-talkies. We had actually been very fortunate earlier in the summer to find a set of four walkie-talkies at a nearby yard sale. A man from our neighborhood had used them on hunting trips to communicate with his hunting partners while out in the woods. He said his hunting days were over, but he was very excited to hear about our new detective agency and was more than happy to sell the hand-held radios to us for a steal.

Scooter handed each of us a radio. If we wanted to keep track of this guy, I guess it would take us splitting up at some point. This way we would be able to keep in touch with each other.

As AJ was putting his radio in his backpack, we heard a loud voice singing, "Love me tender, love me sweet..." His face turned red with embarrassment. AJ reached into his pocket and pulled out his new cell phone. "My mom picked this ringtone." He looked at the screen and laughed. "Speaking of Mom, this is her."

Scooter and I just looked at each other, confused, as AJ answered his phone. We could only hear AJ's side of the conversation, but it sounded like his mom was checking to make sure that he had packed enough water for our biking trip. Then she was worried that he was not wearing any sunscreen. AJ was highly annoyed; he had just seen his mother ten minutes ago at the house, and she was already calling to check on him. He hung up the phone in disgust.

"You know how Mom tends to let me do my own thing? Now that she can get a hold of me whenever she wants, I think that's going to change," he said, holding up the phone in frustration. "So much for 'emergencies only.'"

"Well, AJ is apparently packed appropriately," I joked. "How about you, Scooter? What do you have that is filling up that backpack?"

"I have some of those trackers we have used before. We could stick one on his bicycle; that way we will never lose him. And I also have some other gadgets I have been working on."

"I can't wait to see them in action!" AJ said as he zipped up his backpack and swung it behind him. "So let's get moving!"

"Agreed," said Scooter. Then the three of us took off for the Silverdale YMCA.

CHAPTER 6

Tracking a Traitor

When we got to the Y, it was about 11:30. That left us with a half hour to form a plan before Jerry was scheduled to leave the Y. We realized right away that the tracker was not going to work, at least not yet. All the bicycles were locked up in a metal rack near the entrance to the building. Since the building was almost all glass, there were people running on treadmills inside who were looking directly at the bikes locked up outside. We didn't know what Jerry looked like, so if we were to walk up to the bikes and plant the tracker on his green bike, he could be inside watching us, and we wouldn't even know it. We could not take that chance.

Luckily, of the dozen or so bikes that were locked up, Jerry's was the only green one. The white flames were visible even from a good distance away, so there was no chance of following the wrong bike or kid.

An iron fence surrounded three sides of the large

YMCA parking lot, and a long row of short bushes lined the fourth. The only way Jerry would be able to leave with his bike would be through one of three exits. Unfortunately, since it was summer, the parking lot was fairly crowded, so you couldn't see more than one exit at a time. So the three of us split up to cover the three exits. Scooter took the exit that was closest to the building. He would be able to see Jerry get on his bike when he exited the building and could follow him if he tried to go that way. AJ and I were covering the far exits of the parking lot, so we had to just lay low and listen to our radios for Scooter to tell us what was happening with Jerry.

I found two big trucks parked next to each other with a pretty large gap in between them, so I just rested my bicycle up against the nearby fence and then sat on the curb between the two trucks. I pulled out my radio, told Scooter I was in position, and then prepared for a long wait.

I wondered what this Jerry kid looked like. I thought I remembered reading in her email that Angela was in high school, so I figured if Jerry was her friend, he must be in high school too. I guess I pictured a tall kid with a lot of self-confidence. I mean, you have to be pretty brave to steal something from someone's house, especially when you were invited there!

My thoughts were interrupted by Scooter's voice over the radio. "He is here. And talk about timing, it is exactly noon."

"What's he doing?" I could hear an excited AJ ask over his radio.

"He's unlocking his bike right now," Scooter replied. "Okay, now he's putting on his helmet... putting his backpack on, and now he is getting on his bike... He is looking around. It appears he is looking to see if he is being watched. Don't worry, I am confident he can't see me in my hiding spot... Okay, Ty, looks like he is coming your way."

"Sweet!" My heart started beating a lot faster. "So what is he wearing?"

"Blue helmet, red shirt, and a large black-and-white checkered backpack."

It was only a few seconds later that the kid came zipping past my hiding spot. Jerry was a little shorter than I expected, and if he was hanging out at the Y everyday for two hours, it was not to lift weights. He was pretty scrawny-looking.

I threw my backpack on but stayed in my hiding spot and waited to see which way he would turn out of the parking lot. He took a left. I jumped up and ran over to my bike resting against the fence. "He took a left!" I barked into the radio. Then I hopped onto my bike to follow him.

I was a little worried it would be hard to catch up with Jerry since he had a good head start, but that ended up not being a problem. He actually only rode about a block and stopped at a nearby frozen yogurt shop in a small shopping plaza. In fact, I almost got caught spying on him! I was pedaling as fast as I could to catch up, and when I rounded the corner of a nearby building, Jerry was right there, parking his bike. In order not to attract attention by slamming on the brakes, I just had to zip right on by and circle around the back of all the buildings in the shopping plaza.

Across the parking lot from the yogurt shop were several ugly metal sculptures that had been turned into a circle of fountains. Apparently, it was called *art*. Why someone would pay someone else to make those things was a mystery to me. But they did serve a great purpose: they were large enough for me to hide behind and still have a great view of the yogurt shop. I could see Jerry had taken off his helmet and was showing his dirty-blond hair. He placed his helmet on his bike handlebars. He then leaned his bike up against the window of the yogurt shop.

He looked around, and then he pulled a baseball cap out of his backpack and put it on backwards. He then pulled a large necklace out of the pack and put that on as well. Jerry turned toward the parking lot and took a slow scan of his surroundings. I was almost positive he couldn't see me behind the fountains, but I was a little worried. Jerry's behavior was making me think he thought he was being watched.

I grabbed my radio. "He didn't go far. He went to the yogurt shop just around the corner from the Y. I am watching him from the far side of the parking lot."

"Ten-four. AJ and I will meet you there shortly."

The glare off the windows of the yogurt shop made it hard to see much of what was going on inside, but about three minutes after Jerry had entered the store, I could tell he had sat down at a table against the window, right next to where his bike was parked. Rats! So much for getting a tracker on his bike while he was inside!

Scooter and AJ snuck in behind me. They had taken the long way around in order not to be seen by Jerry.

"So what is he doing?" AJ said before he had even gotten off his bike.

"Eating yogurt, duh! That's him sitting at the table on the other side of the glass from his bike—"

"So no tracker," Scooter interrupted.

"Exactly," I said. "When he got here, though, he was acting really weird. He put on a baseball cap and then what looked like a big gold necklace. And then he looked around, all paranoid, before he went inside."

"That sounds like how he was acting when I saw him come out of the building at the Y," Scooter confirmed. "He is definitely our guy."

"Yup."

"So when he was looking around, did he see you?" Scooter asked accusingly.

"Yeah! I just stood up and waved at him when he looked my way!" I said sarcastically. "Of course not!"

"Okay, okay. Just checking," Scooter said, now on the defensive.

"So what do we do now?" AJ asked impatiently.

"I guess we wait and see where he goes next," Scooter answered.

The three of us sat on the hot pavement for what seemed like a long time, waiting for Jerry to get up from the table and do something, anything. I was starting to get jealous. I would much rather be inside, eating some frozen yogurt, and let someone else bake out in the parking lot, watching *me*!

Suddenly, we heard a familiar voice. "Love me tender, love me sweet…"

AJ's phone was ringing again. Scooter shot him a look. "AJ, what are you doing? That phone is going to get us noticed!"

"Sorry, it's my mom again!" AJ whispered.

"Well, put it on silent next time!"

"Okay, fine." AJ stood up and walked away to answer. "Hi, Mom. What's up?"

"And I thought that phone was going to be a good thing," Scooter grumbled after AJ was out of hearing range.

A few minutes later, AJ returned. "She wanted to know what I wanted for dinner. She is out grocery shopping."

Scooter just groaned.

I looked over and saw that Jerry was standing up from his table. "Hey, guys, here we go!"

Scooter and AJ turned to look just as Jerry was walking out the front door. I expected him to go to his bike, but instead he started to walk down the sidewalk toward the bank a couple doors down. We shuffled a little to our right as he moved to our left, so we would stay hidden behind the sculptures.

Scooter started to dig into his backpack. "Okay, if he goes inside that bank, then, AJ, you take this tracker, run over, and put it under his bike seat. And after you do that, just keep running until you are well out of sight. Then we will radio and tell you where to go pick up your bike, okay?"

"Sure thing, Scoot!" AJ stood up and ran in place to get the blood flowing and prepare for his sprint.

Unfortunately, he did not get the chance to make that sprint. When Jerry got to the bank, he stopped in front of the building and pulled his wallet out of his shorts. Arg! There was an ATM outside the bank, and he was going to use that instead of going inside. From where he was standing, his bike was still within his view.

After using the ATM, Jerry began to walk back to his bike. As he walked, he took off his hat and huge gold necklace and put them in his backpack—but not before looking all around, as usual. He put his helmet on, grabbed his bike, and started to pedal out of the parking lot (luckily, not in our direction). This time all three of us rode together as we followed Jerry, trying to stay a good distance behind.

After awhile, Jerry seemed to be getting tired (I told you he looked sort of wimpy) and was really slowing down. It became hard to follow him because we too had to slow down in order to stay a safe distance behind him. Eventually, Jerry pulled up in front of a pawn shop in Old-Town Silverdale.

"Okay, here we go!" Scooter said excitedly. "He is probably going in there to sell the ruby ring!"

"So what do we do?" AJ asked.

"We wait. Let Jerry sell it. Then we go in and verify it was sold. Then Angela and her grandma come down and prove it belonged to them and was stolen. Then they will alert the police, and Jerry will get what he deserves. Simple as that."

Jerry was inside the store for about five minutes. We decided once again not to try to approach his bike parked out front, because the whole front of the pawn shop was one big glass wall. Man, I guess you never realize how many stores have lots of windows until you try sneaking up on somebody! We decided that I would stick around and talk to the pawn shop after Jerry was gone, and AJ and Scoot would continue to follow Jerry wherever he went next.

As Jerry stepped outside the pawn shop, he looked up to see a city bus—number 33—approaching. He scampered across the street to catch the bus, which had a large rack in front to carry bikes. There were already a couple bikes attached. It took Jerry a long minute to finally get his bike into the rack, and then he jumped on board.

"Come on, let's go!" Scooter said as he turned around and started pedaling away.

I had no clue why we would be running away

or where we were going, but I followed anyway. It wasn't until a minute later that I figured out what Scooter was thinking. The bus passed right by where we had been sitting on our bikes. If we had stayed there, we would have been seen by Jerry for sure. Now the only thing Jerry could have seen was the back of our heads from a good distance away.

After the bus passed by, Scooter turned his bike around and headed toward the bus stop. AJ and I followed, as usual. As we pulled up to the covered bus stop, Scooter asked to himself, "Bus 33, where are you taking our friend Jerry?"

The bus stop had a metal bench for riders to sit and wait. Directly above the bench was a large map showing all the different numbered bus routes. Scooter's finger found the line for 33.

"Jerry got on bus 33. It looks like it actually leads north toward our house. Perhaps he lives near us," he said.

"Yeah, but so do thousands of other people," AJ whined. "We lost him."

"We only lost him today," Scooter said. "Tomorrow, we will pick up his trail again at the Y. Remember, Angela said he is at the Y every day from 10 till 12."

"Oh yeah!" AJ slapped himself in the forehead.

"Now, come on, let's go talk to the pawn shop," Scooter said as he looked both ways and then crossed the street.

The pawn shop owner was a gruff-looking man

with an unkempt beard and the personality of a brick. He did not look like he was interested in answering any questions. He was standing behind the counter, working on fixing a toaster. He barely acknowledged us when we walked in the front door.

It looked like he was our only choice of people to talk to, so I took a big gulp and asked away. "Excuse me, sir, do you have any ruby rings for sale?"

"Nope." The man did not even look up from his toaster.

"Are you sure?" I asked again.

"Are you deaf?" the man replied mockingly.

"I am sorry, sir, it's just that I thought the kid who was just in here about ten minutes ago was trying to sell one, and I figured you bought it. I guess I was wrong."

"I guess you were," the man replied. "If you're talking about the scrawny kid in the red shirt, he wasn't looking to sell anything; he was buying."

"What was he trying to buy?" AJ interrupted excitedly.

"An electric meat slicer—we didn't have one."

"Hmm, okay, thanks."

"Sure. You looking for anything else that I *don't* have?"

"Nope," I said as I quickly left with Scooter and AJ right behind me.

Of course, AJ was the first to speak up once we got outside. "I thought he was trying to sell a stolen ring! Instead, he is looking for a stupid meat slicer?"

"Yeah, I am not sure what this kid is up to," Scooter replied. "Maybe he meant to come in and sell the ring today, but he chickened out at the last minute and asked for something ridiculous instead, just so it looked like he had a valid reason for coming in the store."

"Sounds just crazy enough to be the truth," I said.

"At least we can still pick up the trail tomorrow," Scooter said.

CHAPTER 7
The Great Exchange

The next day we got to the Y a little earlier than the day before. Now that we knew what Jerry looked like, we figured one of us could casually walk down the sidewalk past the row of bikes and see if we saw Jerry inside looking out at the bikes. If he wasn't there, then AJ would walk up with his bike, act like he was going to lock his up next to Jerry's green bike, and then casually plant the tracker under Jerry's bike seat. Great plan, right? Well, not so much. When we got to the Y, we could see that Jerry's green bike wasn't even there!

"Oh great, now what do we do?" complained AJ.

"Let's just wait until noon. He could still be inside. Maybe he decided to walk, or maybe he got a ride today."

"Oh great! So we're going to have to try and follow a car around while we're on bikes!" AJ whined.

"Let's just wait!" Scooter demanded.

AJ and I went to guard the same entrances we

had the day before. Scooter again took lookout. Jerry appeared at the entrance to the Y right at noon. Scooter came on the radio: "He's here, guys. He's looking around… and now he is headed… over to the bicycles?"

"His bike wasn't there," AJ said, confused.

"It looks like he is unlocking a black bike."

"Did he get a new one or something?" I asked.

"I guess so. Okay, he is ready to go. Ty, it looks like he is headed your way again."

"I'm on it," I answered.

This time I didn't have my bike up against the fence like the day before. I kept the bike with me and simply hid behind a large twelve-passenger van. I watched as Jerry once again went flying past me. At the exit to the parking lot, he took a left just like the day before. I got on the radio before I started to follow. "Hey, guys, I have a feeling that Jerry is going to the yogurt place again. He took a left out of the parking lot just like yesterday."

"Okay, AJ and I will meet you in the same spot as yesterday—behind the sculpture fountains. Let us know if you are wrong and he is actually going somewhere else."

I tentatively followed Jerry on my bicycle until he disappeared around the corner near the yogurt shop. I decided not to fly down the road like I had the day before and risk almost running into him again. Instead, I took a different path, which would approach the yogurt shop from the far side.

Sure enough, as I had guessed, Jerry was parking his bike and taking his bike helmet off outside the windows of the yogurt shop. He placed his helmet on his handlebars and then looked around nervously as he opened his backpack. He pulled out a black beret and an expensive-looking purple scarf. He put them on and then entered the store just like the day before.

About the time Jerry sat down to presumably enjoy his yogurt, AJ and Scooter joined me in my stakeout across the parking lot.

"Well, he is in there again. But this time he is wearing a beret and scarf." That got a chuckle out of AJ and Scooter. "Funny, huh?"

"Yeah, I am not sure what you need a scarf for in the middle of summer," Scooter said.

We sat in silence for a minute or two, just staring across the parking lot. Finally, Scooter spoke up again, "You know we really should spread out. I know this parking lot is not that big, but if he comes out and starts heading off somewhere, we should be better prepared to follow him. So, AJ, why don't you work your way over to there—" He pointed at a group of trees across the parking lot. "—and, Tyler, you go to the opposite side. I will stay right here as lookout and report over the radio, just like we did at the Y."

That plan had worked well at the Y, so AJ and I agreed. As soon as I got to my hiding spot, Scooter came on the radio to say that Jerry was on the move.

He said that Jerry was actually headed toward him. I quickly thought about where Jerry might be going. The movie theater, the mall, and the post office were all in that direction. I didn't have to wonder very long.

"Okay, guys, he is going into the mall. He parked his bike near the bookstore entrance. You guys go plant a tracker on his bike. There are lots of bikes in this bike rack, so I am going to leave mine here too. Jerry's black bike is the one to the left of mine. I am going to go inside and follow him around to see what store he goes to. I will keep you posted."

"Ten-four," AJ said immediately.

"Okay, Scoot," I added.

When I arrived at the bookstore entrance to the mall, AJ was already there, sitting on his bike, parked next to Jerry's bike.

"Are you going to plant the tracker?" I asked.

"Already done," AJ said.

"Great. Then let's get out of here before we get spotted."

We rode across the parking lot to a shaded area. While we were riding, Scooter reported that Jerry had gone into a sunglasses store. As we neared the shaded area, we could see a group of about ten skateboarders sitting on the curb about twenty parking spots away. We decided to sit on the curb as well. This way, we wouldn't look suspicious, and we could still keep an eye on Jerry's black bike.

Just as we settled down to listen to Scooter give us more updates on the radio, AJ's phone began to sing, "Love me tender..." He answered quickly as I shot him a dirty look. Again it was his mother, apparently just checking up on him. He hung up with a huff.

"You know, I thought it would be cool to finally have a cell phone, but my mom is driving me crazy. She calls every five minutes! But if I don't answer, she'll start worrying and start freaking out."

Before I could respond, Scooter's voice came over the radio. "Okay, guys, Jerry went into a kitchen store for a minute, and now he is at the jewelry store."

"So he is going to sell the ring!" AJ declared.

"No, these type of stores don't buy jewelry, just sell. I am guessing he is just looking to see what similar rings cost."

We listened for about another half hour as Scooter told us about each and every store Jerry went into—and it was just about *every* store! It appeared that Jerry was just going from one end of the mall to the other, window-shopping as he went. Finally, Scooter came on the radio to tell us that Jerry had entered the department store at the far end of the mall.

"He has been in practically every store in the mall on his way to this one, so I am sure he will be heading back your way shortly."

AJ and I stood for a moment to stretch our legs to get ready for the upcoming chase.

"Uh, guys, he seems to be walking straight through the store. He is not stopping to look at anything. Now he is picking up the pace... Okay, he is walking out the glass doors, and it looks like he is practically jogging. I can't follow him outside, or he will see me. I am going to go out another exit and peek around the building. One sec..."

The radio went silent for a moment while AJ and I just looked at each other in confusion.

"Uh, guys, we have a problem," Scooter said on the radio, clearly out of breath. "He's gone!"

"What do you mean, 'He's gone'?" I yelled into the radio.

"Oh, wait, there he... Oh, man, you guys are not going to believe this. We have lost him."

"What?" AJ and I both said.

"Just ride down to the far side of the mall, and I'll explain." Scooter sounded pretty disappointed. "Oh, wait, my bike is sitting down there. Never mind, I will just meet you back at the bookstore."

"That's okay, Scoot, we'll make it down to you," AJ said, feeling sorry for him. "We'll be there in a sec."

Well, it took us longer than we thought to walk all the way around the mall to where Scooter was sitting and waiting on the curb. It proved to be quite a challenge for either AJ or me to walk two bikes at once.

Scooter started explaining before we even had a chance to ask. "Okay, here's what happened. Jerry came out this exit." He pointed at the doors behind him. "And I had to come out the exit around the corner. By the time I peeked around the corner, Jerry was on his green bike and riding off across the parking lot."

"Wait, did you say his *green* bike?" I asked.

"Yes! He must have had it locked up over there." He pointed to the bike rack to our right. "I couldn't follow him because I didn't have my bike with me, and you guys were all the way on the other side of the mall. No way you could catch him, either!"

"Wow, this guy parks his black bike at one end of the mall, walks through the entire mall, trying to ditch anyone who may be following him, and then picks up a different bike on the other side?" I said, amazed.

"Duuuuuuude, this guy is good!" AJ marveled.

"He's not *that* good," Scooter argued.

"He must have seen us following him," I concluded.

"I don't see how," Scooter said. "We have been very careful. Besides, the guy is clearly just paranoid. He has been looking over his shoulder every five minutes."

"Well, he did steal a ring. Maybe he steals lots of stuff, and he's always worried that someone knows," AJ wondered aloud.

"You know, AJ, you might be on to something there. I could not get close enough to see what he was doing when he went into each store. Maybe he was taking stuff off of the shelves..." Scooter trailed off as he put on his thinking face. He was deep in thought until I interrupted.

"So do we pick up the trail again tomorrow at the Y at noon?" I said with a chuckle.

"I guess we are going to have to," Scooter said as he hopped on his bike and headed toward home.

CHAPTER 8

The Return of Sherlock Holmes

The next morning was the third day of following Jerry. In anticipation of Jerry keeping up his pattern, we decided one of us should go inside the yogurt shop ahead of Jerry to observe him inside. AJ was very quick to volunteer, of course! We figured if AJ was already inside when Jerry arrived, Jerry would not be suspicious. After all, AJ couldn't really be accused of following him if he was there before him.

Meanwhile, over at the YMCA, Scooter and I waited. There wasn't a green or a black bike sitting in front of the building. We had figured the black one wouldn't be there. After all, AJ had put the tracker under the seat. When Scooter checked it in the morning, the computer program said it hadn't moved from the bookstore. We hoped this didn't mean that Jerry had broken his pattern. He did not disappoint.

At twelve o'clock on the dot, Jerry walked out the front of the Y with his black-and-white checkered backpack slung over his shoulders. Jerry did not walk over to the bike rack at all this time. He walked right into the parking lot. It became pretty clear that he was indeed going to the yogurt shop because he was walking toward it in the most direct way possible—weaving in between cars instead of staying on the sidewalks or aisles of the parking lot. Scooter and I circled around to our usual spot behind the fountains to observe him from a safe distance. As Jerry neared the parking lot, he reached into his backpack and pulled out a large, floppy hat and large, wide sunglasses. He put them on and then entered the shop. He filled a cup of yogurt, paid, and then sat in his usual chair by the window.

We could see AJ sitting a few tables away, also eating a cup of yogurt and trying to look busy by reading one of the newspapers that someone had left behind early in the day. Suddenly, AJ started digging in his pocket. His phone must have been ringing! He pulled it out, talked for about ten seconds, and hung up. He then shot a look through the window in our direction. He could probably feel Scooter shooting him dirty looks all the way across the parking lot. He deserved it, though; he was going to blow his cover!

After about twenty minutes, Jerry got up, went outside, and started walking in a direction he had not been the previous two days. As he walked, he took off the ridiculous hat and sunglasses and put those back in his backpack. It was actually hard to follow him because he was walking and we had our bikes with us. We basically had to stay two blocks behind him, walking our bikes in order not to catch up with him. AJ took a little longer than I thought he would, but he eventually caught up with Scooter and me. He immediately went on to explain what had taken so long.

"So Jerry went in the store and ordered his yogurt using an Australian accent. Then when he sat down, he started talking to himself, and every once in a while, he would speak to the other people in the shop with the same accent, saying stuff like, 'G'day, Mate,' and, 'My pet koala,' and other weird stuff."

"Uh, yeah, that is weird," I said as the three of us walked down the street.

"It gets weirder. So after Jerry left, I joked with the lady behind the counter and said, 'Sort of a weird guy, wasn't he?' And she told me that he comes in almost every day with a different costume and speaks with a horrible matching accent. The people that work there actually have a contest each day to see who can be the first to guess what he is trying to be."

"Hmm. You think he is some sort of actor?" I asked.

"If so, he's a bad one," AJ said. "You should have heard him. On second thought, be glad you didn't!"

"So what was up with the phone call?" Scooter demanded. "I thought we told you to put the phone on silent!"

"I did, but it was my mom again. If I don't answer, she'll freak out and worry."

"Boy, that phone seems like more trouble than it is worth," Scooter said.

"Maybe you need to teach your mom how to text," I joked.

"Not a bad idea," Scooter added.

"Yeah, yeah, yeah." AJ brushed us off as we continued walking our bikes a safe distance behind Jerry. After about twenty minutes of walking, Jerry left the sidewalk and cut across a parking lot.

"Hey, it looks like Jerry is going into the S-G-S!" AJ pointed to Jerry, who was walking in the front door of the store.

"I think one of us needs to go inside the store to see what he is doing," Scooter said.

"That store is so crowded, I think all of us could go in and blend in just fine," I argued.

"No, AJ can't go," Scooter said. "Jerry has probably already seen him in the yogurt shop. It would be too risky. Aidge, you stay out here and keep lookout. Besides, someone has to watch our bikes, anyway."

AJ reluctantly agreed, and so while he watched the entrance of the S-G-S, Scooter and I entered the front door, trying to act as normal as possible.

The S-G-S stood for Still Good Stuff. It was a store where you could buy used *anything* for a huge discount! Used clothes, used furniture, used toys and books, and my favorite—used video games! I actually visited the S-G-S quite often, but today the store seemed more crowded than usual. Maybe because it was Saturday. Dozens of conversations filled the store with a sound like a gigantic bumblebee. The strong smells of tuna fish and cinnamon drifted through the air—two scents that did not mix well. The summer heat and all the people made the place really warm too.

Scooter went to the right, and I went to the left. After only a couple aisles, I spotted Jerry. He was looking at the shelves of used books. I walked right past that aisle and then quickly circled back around to the far end of the same aisle. That way I could watch him from a safer distance while I pretended to browse the shelves.

Jerry seemed to be looking for a particular book. Out of the corner of my eye, I saw him pull a small piece of paper out of his pocket. He read it and then looked at the books again. He pulled a book off the shelves that for some reason looked familiar to me. The size and color of the book made me think I had seen it before. Maybe I had seen it on the bookshelves of my home or something; I was too far away to read what the cover said. Although it was bothering me, I was not about to get closer just to satisfy my curiosity and risk being spotted by Jerry.

Jerry pulled the small piece of paper out one more time and mouthed the words he was reading. He put the paper back in his pocket and then began flipping through the book in his hand. I realized he was looking for a specific page. When he found the right page he just stared at the opened book for a moment, and then he reached into his other pocket and pulled out a red envelope. He look around to see if anyone was watching (I pulled a book off the shelf and pretended to read the back cover), and then he put the red envelope into the open book. He closed the book and put it back on the shelf. He looked at his wristwatch. Then he headed directly for the exit.

I quickly pulled my walkie-talkie out of my pocket. "AJ, he is coming out of the store now! Scooter, come meet me in the book aisle." I didn't move. By staying still, I hoped to memorize where Jerry had put the book on the shelves.

Scooter came up next to me. "What happened, Ty?"

"Jerry took a red envelope out of his pocket, put it in one of the used books, and then put the book back on the shelf," I said.

"That's weird" is all Scooter said as he put on his thinking face.

"That's what I thought. Why would he do that?"

"Not sure. Let's go take a look," Scooter said, already walking down the aisle. "About where did he put this book? This is a lot of books to look through."

At that moment I was rather proud of myself for thinking ahead and memorizing the general location of the book. "It's on the top shelf, in the second section over from the end of the aisle."

I began scanning books in that section, looking

for a dark brown leather book. Scooter also began to search, although I was not sure what he was looking for, since he hadn't seen Jerry with the book.

Just then AJ came on the radio, "Guys, Jerry is waiting at the bus stop, and the bus is about to get here. I can't follow him because I am watching three bikes! We're about to lose him again!"

Scooter reached up and grabbed a book off the shelf. He then took the walkie-talkie I was holding. "Don't worry about it, Aidge. We have everything we need right here." Scooter opened the book he was holding, and stuffed inside was the red envelope!

"How did you know which book it was?" I asked in shock. "I didn't even tell you what it looked like!"

Scooter took the envelope out and then closed the book to show me the spine. It read *The Return of Sherlock Holmes*. "This book is the sequel to the book that A.F. sent me during our last case. It can't be a coincidence that this book just happens to be in the near vicinity of where we were searching. Plus, look at how nice this book is, compared to all the ones around it. It sticks out like a sore thumb." He flipped it over to show that the pages were lined with gold, which made the book look rather expensive.

"I knew that book looked familiar for some reason when I saw Jerry holding it!" In *The Case of the Bike in the Birdcage*, Scooter had been given an expensive copy of *The Adventures of Sherlock Holmes*; it looked like this one might be the second part of the same set. Inside the first book had been a code left for us by A.F.—our first introduction to the mysterious initials. That must mean that A.F. was leaving someone a message, and we had stumbled across it! Scooter and I looked up at each other at the exact same time. I think we were both coming to that same realization. Scooter tossed me the book and began to rip open the red envelope. Inside were five pages of looseleaf paper containing tons of numbers. Most of them were in pairs separated by a dash. We had seen this code before.

"It looks like we intercepted a message from A.F.," I said excitedly.

"No, I bet you this message was intended for us. We didn't intercept anything," Scooter said. "These pairs of numbers are just like the type A.F. sent us in the first message, and this book is just like that one. This is too similar to be just a coincidence."

In our previous case, we had eventually figured out that the pairs of numbers were like an address. If you were looking at the page of a book, and the code said 7–9, then you were supposed to find the seventh line of the book and then count the ninth letter on that line. So 7–9 would represent a single letter. Find all the letters, put them together, and they form words and maybe even sentences.

Only one problem: the code worked for just one specific page. In this case I had no clue what page we were supposed to be on. Maybe Scooter knew. "So what page do we use to solve the number code?"

"I am not sure," Scooter said as he began flipping

through the book, looking for a clue.

"Uh-oh, Scoot, I think you messed up."

"What do you mean?" Scooter asked defensively.

"Well, when I was watching Jerry, he looked like he was looking for a specific page before putting the envelope in the book. I think the envelope was marking the page we were supposed to use. You took the envelope out and then shut the book, so now we've lost our place."

"Oh no! Well, it was about in the middle," he said hopefully.

"That's a pretty thick book! Being 'about in the middle' still leaves a lot of possibilities," I said.

"Yeah, you're right, Ty. We are going to have to take this home and figure it out later." He took the book and headed toward the front of the store. "We had better hope that this book doesn't cost more than five bucks. That's all I have!"

Scooter got in line to check out. The wait looked like it might be long. Then an employee tapped Scooter on the shoulder and explained she was opening a new checkout line. She would be glad to ring him up, if he would like. Scooter happily accepted. The book, even though it looked so nice, was only $2.99. What a steal of a deal! Even the checker thought so. She kept pointing out what a great bargain Scooter was getting. Boy, do I love the S-G-S!

When Scoot and I left the store, an impatient AJ was waiting. "Jerry got on the 33 bus again. In case anyone wanted to know," he snapped. He frowned when he saw the book under Scooter's arm. "I am out here, freaking out about losing Jerry, and you two bozos are in there shopping for books?"

"Not just any book. We think we got another message from A.F. inside!" I said proudly.

AJ's anger turned to curiosity. "Really? Well, what did he say?"

"We don't know yet; we have to decode it first," Scooter answered.

"Then how do you know it's from him?"

Not wanting to explain it all over again, Scooter just said, "You will just have to trust me. But let's go, and I will prove it to you."

CHAPTER 9
A Familiar Foe

We went straight from the S-G-S to Scooter's house. We dumped our bikes in the driveway, ran around behind the house, and made our way down to HQ. Once we got there, Scooter grabbed a chair and sat down at the small table. He asked me to grab some blank printer paper for scribbling on. Meanwhile, AJ grabbed a banana off the counter and decided to stay out of the way and eat. (Doesn't that sound like what he always does?)

Scooter was confident that the red envelope had been placed pretty close to the middle of the book. The book was 400 pages long, so Scooter started at page 200 and then went backward 30 pages to 170. He took the pieces of paper from the red envelope and began to decode the message using page 170. The first ten letters were GFIZPPRWDG. Clearly, page 170 wasn't the right one. He did the same thing for page 171 and got similar junk results. He continued this method for about 40 pages until he came to page 213. As he started to decode the first group of letters, it spelled GREETINGS. Scooter and I got excited: we had found an actual word! Scooter decoded the entire first line of the note. It read *GREETINGS ENIGMA SQUAD,*.

"We got it!" Scooter announced.

"You got the message?" AJ asked from the computer, where he had started playing (and losing) a world-domination strategy game. "What does it say?"

"I don't know; I am still working on it." Scooter then spent the next five minutes working as fast as he possibly could, decoding the message as AJ and I impatiently waited for him to finish. When Scooter was done decoding the entire message, he leaned back in his chair so all three of us could read what was written on the piece of printer paper.

Greetings Enigma Squad,

I see that Jerry has delivered my message to you. By the way, don't be too mad at him. He didn't actually do anything wrong—like steal a ring or anything. I just sent him on a wild goose chase. Poor guy, wandering around town, not really sure what he was doing. Sort of reminds me of some other kids I know! Oh, what joy it brought me to watch the three of you running around town, trying to keep up. I must say, I thought after our last encounter that I had found a worthy opponent, but alas, I was apparently wrong. The Enigma Squad is no match for me. So it is with deep sadness that I must say goodbye. It was quite fun while it lasted.

Yours truly,

A.F.

P.S. Angela Fitzpatrick says hello.

AJ was the first to speak up. "So A.F. knows Angela Fitzpatrick, huh?"

"No, dummy, A.F. *is* Angela Fitzpatrick," Scooter scolded. "Well, not really. A.F. made her up. I can't believe I did not see it sooner! You realize Angela's initials are A.F.?"

"He left us a clue from the very beginning, and we missed it!" I said.

"Wait, so I am confused. If they're the same, then why did he—or she—hire us?" AJ asked.

"I think A.F. just wanted to see how easily he could mess with us," I said.

"It was obviously pretty easy!" AJ said. "We fell for his trick like a bunch of fools!"

"So do you really think he is saying goodbye?" I asked.

"I don't know, this might just be another one of his games," Scooter said. "Whether he thinks he is done with us or not, it doesn't matter. We are definitely not done with him."

"Yeah, but A.F. always contacts us. How are we going to track him down?" AJ asked.

Scooter and I looked at each other, and then we said in near unison: "Jerry!"

"If A.F. was telling Jerry what to do, then we track down Jerry and work backward to find A.F.," Scooter added.

"So where do you think the best place to catch Jerry is?" I asked.

"I think we have to try the YMCA and yogurt shop again."

"You really think he'll go back to those places again?" AJ asked. "Like A.F. said, he's done messing with us. So he won't be sending Jerry there anymore."

"But how do we know A.F. sent Jerry to those places? Maybe that is just where Jerry normally goes. Anyway, I don't have any better ideas. I think we have to at least check them out tomorrow."

"Fine," said the rarely pessimistic AJ, "but I bet he won't be there."

The next day was Sunday. I had church to attend in the morning, so we decided to meet at the YMCA as soon as we possibly could the next day. Hopefully, we could all get there before noon so we wouldn't miss Jerry exiting the building.

The next day at church was painful. Usually, I really get into what the preacher has to say, but I have to confess that this particular Sunday, all I could think about was how long before we could get out and get home. After the sermon, I impatiently waited for my parents to finish their friendly conversations so I could nudge them in the direction of our car. Overall, my strategy worked. We got home at 11:30.

I quickly changed my clothes and pedaled my bike as fast as I could down the hill toward town. I got to the YMCA, where Scooter and AJ were waiting, with ten minutes to spare. We hoped that day would be our last day of trying to track Jerry, so we decided to split up again to cover more area and be sure to catch him. AJ and I watched the entrance to the YMCA, while Scooter set up in our usual spot across from the yogurt shop.

AJ and I had a couple minutes to wait, so we went and checked out the bikes in front of the Y. Once again, there wasn't a bike that we recognized as belonging to Jerry. Things did not look promising for Jerry to be here. Sure enough, twelve o'clock came and went with still no sign of him. A ton of sweaty people flooded out the doors around 12:10, and Jerry was not in that group, either. Finally, we radioed Scooter to tell him it did not appear that Jerry had gone to the Y as usual. Scooter reported back that there was no sign of Jerry on his end, either. He told us to give up and meet him over at the yogurt shop.

When AJ and I got to our usual spot behind the sculpture fountains, Scooter was nowhere to be seen. We looked around the parking lot for any sign of him. Still nothing. Then we saw Scooter walk out of the yogurt shop, eating a bowl of frozen yogurt.

"Scooter, what are you doing?" AJ demanded.

A big smile came across Scooter's face. "Hey, I figured you got some dessert yesterday, so I deserve some today!"

"I mean, what are you doing blowing your cover and going inside the yogurt shop!" AJ said.

"I know what you meant." Scooter continued his knowing smile. "I just figured that if Jerry had not shown up by now, then he was not going to at all."

"Man, another dead end!" AJ complained.

"Not exactly. While I was inside, I asked the girl serving yogurt what she knew about Jerry, and she told me pretty much the same thing we had already heard from AJ. Apparently, Jerry comes in with a different outfit every day, and he seems to be practicing a different accent too. But here is the good news: Jerry was actually already here today when they opened at ten—"

"Since he didn't have to go to the Y anymore, he could come early!" I interrupted.

"Exactly!" Scooter was getting more excited; I could tell because he was hopping from foot to foot. "And here is the best part. The girl said that when she showed up to open the store, Jerry was outside. He was wearing all camouflage and was sitting on his black bike waiting to come in."

"Did you say *black* bike?" I asked.

"He did!" AJ answered for him.

"So I think we need to hurry up and get back to HQ to check my computer for where that tracker has gone. Let's hope it is still stuck to the bottom of the seat!"

AJ and I hopped on our bikes and were anxious to race home but we had to sit patiently for Scooter to scoop every last ounce of frozen yogurt out of his cup before we could go. The ride up the hill to our neighborhood was almost unbearable. As I slowly pedaled, I hoped some huge wind would suddenly start blowing at my back and rush me the rest of the way up the hill. We were keeping a steady pace, but AJ, who was in the lead, stopped on the shoulder of the road and forced us to stop behind him. He dug his cell phone out of his pocket and stared at the screen.

"What now?" Scooter asked in frustration.

"I got a text," AJ said, excited. But then he realized who it was from. "Oh, it's from my mom. She wants to know what time I'll be home for dinner."

"Well, at least she stopped calling you," I offered.

"Yeah, I guess this is a little better." He made us wait as he sent his mother a reply text. After a painful minute of watching AJ type, then delete, then type again, we finally headed up the rest of the hill.

When we got to Scooter's house, we ditched our bikes on the front lawn and ran around to the back of the house. Since it was the middle of the day, we decided to be cautious and take the Straight-a-Way entrance to HQ. The entrance was deep enough in the woods that there wasn't really a risk of being seen that way.

Once we got inside HQ, AJ and I hovered above Scooter while he loaded up the computer program that mapped out where the tracker had been. On the screen was a map of Silverdale and the surrounding areas. Scooter had things set up so every thirty seconds, it would display a new glowing green dot representing the updated location of the tracker. If he clicked on any one of those dots, it would tell him what time that dot was created.

With a few clicks of the mouse, Scooter was able to discover that Jerry's bike had not moved from the mall bookstore for the past couple days. But then this morning around 9:45, the bike moved. It moved directly over to the yogurt shop.

Then at 10:30, it went back over to the mall bookstore again.

"Strange," Scooter muttered.

"So he was at the mall, went over and got yogurt when they opened the store, and then went back to hanging out at the mall?" I asked.

"It looks like it," Scooter said. He then went back to following the history of the tracker. It appeared that the tracker had stayed at the mall until about 1:20. Then it left and went directly north. It headed up the same hill we had just climbed, but it stopped at the entrance to Hidden Place and had been sitting there since 1:40.

"1:40?" I said. "What time is it now?"

"1:45."

I was excited. "That means Jerry has only been at that location for five minutes! C'mon, if we hurry, we should be able to catch him."

"We can hurry, but I don't think we need to."

"Why not?" I said, trying to get AJ and Scooter to follow me out the door.

"I think Jerry lives there. He's not going anywhere."

"Hey, isn't Hidden Place the same street that the haunted Safari House is on?" asked AJ. "Maybe after we catch Jerry, I can ask him if has seen the monkeys."

"Oh my goodness, not this again!" Scooter moaned. He stood up to join me at the door. AJ went over to the bowl of fruit by the sink, took a moment to decide, and then grabbed an apple and shoved it into his mouth. He bit down to hold it there. This gave him two free hands to push the massive vault door shut behind us.

CHAPTER 10
The Tiger on the Toilet

The bike ride down the hill toward Hidden Place was faster and much more fun than the ride uphill a bit earlier. Once we got there, we were going to have to figure out which of the houses near the entrance to Hidden Place belonged to Jerry. The computer could only narrow down the location of the tracker to that general area. We would have to narrow it down further from there.

When we turned onto Hidden Place, though, we immediately realized that our search was going to be easy. The black bike was sitting in the driveway of the house to our left. I was about to ask what the plan was when the front door to the house opened, and out walked Jerry! He closed the door behind him and then used a key to lock it.

AJ yelled at the kid, "Hey, Jerry, we need to talk to you!"

Jerry was startled and stumbled down the few stairs in front of the house. He looked at us and then quickly scrambled to his feet. He took off in a sprint up the hill. AJ pushed his bike over into the grass on the side of the street and started running after him. Jerry had a good head start, but I was confident that AJ could catch him. I dropped my bike next to AJ's and started chasing after both Jerry and AJ. Scooter took a second and then decided to do the same. The hill was very steep, and I was out of breath after only a few seconds.

"Keep going, AJ! You have to catch him!" I said as I bent over to try and catch my breath. "He is the only clue we've got right now!" I huffed and puffed with my hands resting on my knees as I watched AJ continue sprinting up the hill, chasing after the kid.

Scooter caught up with me but didn't stop; he just gave a breathy, "Come on, Ty," as he continued his steady-paced jog up the hill, following AJ.

Now if any of this sounds familiar, it is because, way back when I started my report, I started telling you about this uphill chase. So let me fast-forward and get you to the good part.

We chased Jerry to the top of the hill. Crazy Jerry went inside the old Safari House! Although AJ was against it, the three of us followed Jerry inside. Jerry seemed to disappear into thin air, but then we heard noises upstairs. They were coming from behind a closed door. Once we got upstairs, AJ yanked the door open.

We looked into the small bathroom and froze in

fright. Standing on the lid to the toilet was the biggest tiger I had ever seen! It was caught by surprise by the door opening so quickly. The tiger turned its body on the toilet lid in order to face us. It snarled, showing its huge, yellow teeth. The tiger bent his legs and gripped the toilet bowl with his front paws. It was about to pounce!

AJ yelled, "Run!" and tried to swing the door closed. We scrambled toward the stairs. I heard a loud *sccrraaaatch* and then a *CRASH* behind us. I glanced toward the bathroom. The bathroom door had been flung open so quickly that it had slammed into the wall behind it. I could see claw marks carved straight down the inside of the bathroom door. The tiger must have put its front paws on the door, and the tiger's massive weight had caused the door to fly open. The tiger was now moving through the doorway! I turned away and focused on the stairs.

At the bottom of the stairs, we turned around to see the tiger already perched at the top. It snarled and again showed us those huge, yellow teeth as it looked down at us. Almost frozen in fear, we slowly began to inch our way backward toward the safety of the front door. Neither we nor the tiger could take our eyes off each other. I don't know a lot about tigers, but I am pretty sure this one could leap down the entire flight of steps in one giant leap. I was behind AJ and Scoot, and my hands fumbled behind me, reaching to find the doorknob that would save us. As we continued our slow, backward shuffle across the entryway, the tiger's eyes followed us intently. It was like he was considering if the meal in front of him was really worth the effort. Finally, my hand felt the doorknob.

I whispered, "Let's get outta here."

I turned the doorknob slowly, until the front door was free and started to open inward slightly. The three of us froze as the door creaked, and the tiger's ears twitched. Then in one motion, I pulled the door open toward me with my right hand and spun, shoving Scooter around it and out of the house with my left. AJ never stopped moving; he shot right out the front door after Scooter. I followed right behind. The tiger had taken a couple curious steps down the stairs. I did not wait around to see what it would do next. I slammed the front door and sprinted to catch up with AJ and Scooter, who were already halfway down the driveway.

We ran right down the middle of the street and didn't look back until we reached the first bend in the road. At that point, since we hadn't been chased down and eaten, we felt like it was finally safe and stopped to regroup.

"Okay, now THAT was real!" Scooter said.

"You won't ever doubt me again!" AJ said proudly.

"Well, I wouldn't go that far," Scooter laughed.

"What in the world is a tiger doing in the bathroom?" I asked.

"Hey, when you gotta go, you gotta go!" AJ joked. We all laughed nervously at first and then louder and more freely. It seemed like a great way to calm our nerves.

"Okay, so now do you believe me? I told you that house was haunted!" AJ said.

"For the last time, the house is not haunted," Scooter argued. "That was not a ghost! That was a real, living-and-breathing tiger! Did you not hear the *crash* it made when it pawed open the bathroom door?"

"I'm wondering what happened to Jerry," I said. "He went in that house, and we didn't see him come out!"

"He could still be in the house!" Scooter said. "He could be stuck in there with a tiger!"

"Or maybe the tiger already got him!" AJ said.

"Let's not jump to that conclusion, AJ. Hey! Do you have your phone handy? I would say this qualifies as an emergency, wouldn't you?"

"Yeah." AJ dug into his pocket and pulled out his phone. Scooter grabbed it without asking and dialed 911.

"Hello. I am at 1711 Hidden Place, and I need police help immediately. A boy just entered the house, and there is also a tiger inside. Yes, a tiger. No, this is not a prank call! Tell Commander Coleman this is Scooter Parks; he will vouch for me. I am not making this up! Hurry!" He hung up the phone without allowing the operator on the other end to respond.

AJ and I looked at him in shock.

"What? She wasn't going to believe me, even if I

kept on talking! Now she will send someone out to check our story because she can't be sure one way or the other."

Scooter handed AJ back the phone, and we began to wait. Suddenly, I saw motion from the corner of my eye. I looked over to my left, and there was Jerry, walking out of the woods! I whispered and pointed, "Hey, guys! There's Jerry." All three of us looked that way.

"Hey!" AJ yelled. Jerry looked over in our direction and immediately turned around and ran back into the woods.

"You know, if you keep yelling at him, we are never going to catch him," Scooter scolded.

"Well, at least we know he is safe, and the tiger didn't get him," I pointed out.

"What do we do now?" AJ asked. "Should we chase him?"

"I don't think we are going to be able to catch Jerry right now. I think we need to stay right here and wait for the police. I gave them my name, so if Commander Coleman shows up here, he is going to be looking for us."

AJ reluctantly agreed to wait, and soon the topic changed to wondering just how Jerry could have escaped from the house. None of us remembered seeing a back door to the house, and we would have seen him if he had walked out the front door. We were still trying to figure it out when a police car came zipping around the corner and screeched to a halt next to us. It was Commander Coleman. He saw that all three of us were there and looked confused.

"I thought you said one of you boys was in trouble. And was there also something about a tiger?"

"No, sir, we are fine. There was a kid whom we were following, and he went into that house." Scooter pointed toward the Safari House. "He somehow got out of the house safely, but it wasn't until after I had called 911. But there is also a tiger, and it is still in the house!"

"A tiger?" Coleman asked with skepticism.

"Yes!" we said in unison.

"Seriously? Well, let's go check it out, then!" He moved the car into the driveway of the old Safari House and then got out. He noticed that none of us had moved from our spot down the hill.

"Aren't you guys coming?" he joked.

Clearly, he did not believe our story. He was still being cautious, though, because he pulled a large gun out of the back of his car. We watched as he loaded two bright orange darts into the gun—tranquilizer darts is what I assumed. Coleman also grabbed a flashlight from inside his car, and then he shut the door. He slowly approached the house. He walked over and peeked into the windows for a while. Then, he quietly walked over to the front door, slowly opened it, and disappeared inside.

CHAPTER 11
Another Head-Scratcher

Have you ever had one of those experiences when it seems like time stands still? Well, this was one of those times. Every minute that Commander Coleman was inside that house seemed to take forever. AJ and Scooter just stared at the front door to the old Safari House, waiting for Coleman to appear. I couldn't bear to watch. I just paced back and forth in the street. I was about to tell AJ to dig his phone back out because we were going to have to call 911 again, but then Commander Coleman walked out the front door. He noticed his head and shoulders were covered in cobwebs and began to pull them off. He looked up and waved for the three of us to come to him. I was a little nervous to do so. But he was still alive and in one piece, so I figured it was safe to approach his car in the driveway.

"I'm not sure what you guys are trying to do, but calling 911 is not a laughing matter," he scolded.

"But, sir, we were not joking—" Scooter began,

but Coleman cut him off.

"You say you were chasing a kid, but there is no kid. You say you were being chased by a tiger, but there is no tiger."

AJ and I looked at each other, scratching our heads, but Scooter started walking toward the front door. "There has to be proof of a tiger in there somewhere..."

Coleman stuck his hand out to stop Scooter. "I'm sorry, boys, but you have already wasted enough of my time. It's too bad I can't make you three do the paperwork you've caused me. If you know what's good for you, you'll turn around and head home. Now." He gently grabbed Scooter by the shoulders and turned him around to face downhill. "Now, get home!"

Dejected, we walked out of the driveway and headed downhill toward our bikes. Commander Coleman gave us a halfhearted wave as he drove by, heading back to the station. When we got to the bottom of the hill and grabbed our bikes, I noticed that Jerry's bike was gone from the driveway it was sitting in earlier. There was now a blue sedan in the driveway.

"Hey, guys, it looks like Jerry must have come home and then taken off on his bike again." I pointed at the driveway.

"And now someone else is home," Scooter said as he began to walk his bike over to the house.

"What are you doing?" I asked, chasing after him.

"I am going to find out what time Jerry is coming

home." He smiled.

He walked up the front steps and knocked on the door. AJ and I hesitantly followed. After about thirty seconds, a young woman a little more than twenty years old answered the door. She wore a white collared shirt and black pants, and it was obvious she was a waitress at a diner in Silverdale because she was still wearing her nametag, which read *Fifi*.

Hmm, interesting, I thought.

"Hello?" Fifi said, obviously wondering what the three of us boys were doing at her doorstep. She probably thought we were selling something.

"Uh, hi... Fifi?" Scooter said, reading her tag. "Is Jerry home?"

"What? There is no Jerry here! And how do you know my nickname?" Fifi asked suspiciously.

"Uh, because..." Scooter pointed at Fifi's shirt, where her nametag was pinned.

"Oh, yeah," Fifi laughed at herself. "The name is actually Felicia."

"Okay, Felicia. Are you sure there is not a Jerry who lives here?"

I wanted to reach up and smack Scooter for such a dumb question. Obviously, Fifi—or Felicia—would know who lives at her house. I jumped in to rescue Scooter before he made an even bigger embarrassment of himself.

"We just made a new friend named Jerry, and we thought he lived here because we saw him come outside and lock the front door."

"Oh, you're talking about Jayjay. That's what I call him. He's a sweet kid, but no, he doesn't live here. I just asked him to stop by and keep an eye on my dog, Cici. She's expecting puppies any day now. With my job, I work lots of weird hours, and I just know my precious Cici is going to have those babies while I'm stuck at work!"

What is up with this girl and the nicknames? I thought.

"Oh, okay," Scooter said, satisfied.

AJ jumped in with a question of his own. "We're also wondering if Jerry has been acting strange lately. Has he been acting differently?"

Felicia appeared to be getting suspicious. "Wait, what's with all these questions?" Then, suddenly, as if a thought had just clicked in her head, she lowered her voice. "Wait a sec, are you guys trying to become junior-level spies too? Is this all part of your training?"

"Excuse me?" I said.

"What are you talking about?" Scooter asked.

"So you aren't training to be spies, then?" she asked.

"No," I said, "we don't know anything about spies."

"Huh," she said. "Well, clearly you need to get to know Jayjay better. I'd say he hasn't been any weirder than normal."

"What do you mean?" I asked.

"Jayjay has always been a little weird as long as

I've known him. I used to babysit him when he was little, and for as long as I can remember, he's been, like, obsessed with everything spy-related. Always reading some new spy novel, making up secret codes, watching spy movies I've never even heard of. Totally obsessed with the stuff. Then a few days ago, he tells me that he was actually approached by the CIA and is being actively recruited to join as a junior-level spy."

"Seriously?" Scooter asked in disbelief.

"Yeah, I thought it sounded like another one of his spy-game scenarios or something, but then he showed me a business card he got from the guy. It looked like it was pretty real. Anyway, Jayjay said he was 'on assignment' for the next few days, whatever that means. I don't really care as long as he can still check on Cici for me."

We all looked at each other in confusion. Something was starting to click in my head, but I couldn't quite put it together.

"Yeah, clearly we need to get to know Jerry better," Scooter joked. "So if Jerry doesn't live here, where does he live?"

She looked up the hill and began to answer and then stopped herself. "Y'know, this conversation is starting to make me feel uncomfortable. I think I've shared too much. I'm gonna have to ask you to leave." She backed away from the doorway so she could close the front door.

"Well, thanks. We're sorry to have bothered you,"

I apologized as we began to back down the steps.

Now Felicia became the one to apologize. "Oh, it's no problem. I'm sorry, it's just that I have to go look after Cici..." She trailed off as she shut the door.

As we walked down the driveway, Scooter began to think out loud, "Okay, so Jerry thinks he's a—"

He was interrupted by a familiar voice. "Love me tender, love me sweet..."

Scooter gave AJ yet another dirty look. AJ shrugged his shoulders and looked at the screen. He rolled his eyes and said, "It's my mom again."

Has anyone other than your mom ever called you? I asked myself.

AJ answered the phone, "Hey, mom, what's up?" Trying not to let his annoyance show in his voice, he walked a few steps away from us to speak to her. Scooter and I stood in silence, waiting for AJ, not wanting to discuss anything without him. (We would just have to repeat ourselves when he joined us, anyway.)

AJ walked back over to us, still holding the phone by his ear. "Mom is making sticky chicken and rice tonight. Do you want to join us for dinner?"

Scooter and I both said *yes* without hesitation. Sticky chicken is one of the most delicious dinners I have ever tasted. I don't know how to describe it; I guess it's like chicken nuggets, smothered in honey and other sweet stuff—I have no clue what—and then all that poured over rice. It's basically candy for dinner!

"Yeah, they're in," AJ said into the phone. "Yeah, we'll be there in ten minutes. Love you, Mom. Bye." He hung up the phone and smiled.

Scooter was confused. "Ten minutes? Doesn't sticky chicken take a really long time to make? Why did you say we would be there in ten minutes? We have a ton of stuff to discuss."

"Yeah, about that... Our discussion will have to wait; we have some work to do first. I sort of volunteered you both," AJ said, shrugging his shoulders in apology.

"What?" I demanded an explanation.

"Well, my mom said she would fix sticky chicken for us if we would help her rearrange the downstairs furniture. So let's go!"

"Wait a minute," said an irritated Scooter. He was not happy about having to move the downstairs furniture—again.

Mrs. Seeva liked to rearrange her living room every couple months, and one time the three of us were asked to help her. It was a nightmare. It took her forever to make up her mind! She would say, "Move the couch over by the window." So we would. Then she would decide she liked it better over by the fireplace. So we would move it over there. Then she would decide she liked it better by the window, and we would move it back to the window again. You would never think that rearranging a living room could be so exhausting!

"I didn't mention the furniture part earlier

because you would have said *no*," AJ explained.

"You're absolutely right: we would have said no!" Scooter said. Not even sticky chicken was worth that pain and suffering.

"And then I would have been stuck doing it myself, and I would have been miserable. So now misery has company!" he said with a smile, smacking us both on our backs. He jumped on his bike and started pedaling away. Scooter and I groaned, but we reluctantly picked up our bikes and followed him toward home.

On the way to AJ's house, I stopped by my house to ask my mom if it was okay if I missed our typical six o'clock dinner.

"Hey, Mom. Is it okay if I don't make it for dinner at six? Mrs. Seeva asked us if we would help her move some furniture."

"Oh sure, honey, that will be fine. What time do you think you will get home, then?"

"I would say around eight," I guessed.

"Okay, we will see you then. Tyler, I just have to tell you that I am so proud of you. That is so sweet that you are willing to sacrifice dinner to help her out."

I decided not to mention the fact that I was getting one of my favorite meals out of the deal. Mom sounded so surprised by my act of kindness that I didn't want to disappoint her with the truth.

The moving furniture part was not as bad this time because Mrs. Seeva was attempting to cook and bark instructions to us at the same time. We basically moved stuff around the living room the entire time she was cooking, and then she decided the way it looked would "have to do" since dinner was ready. We boys shared a quiet laugh because the living room actually looked almost identical to when we started!

I had built up quite an appetite and Mrs. Seeva had made extra, so I proceeded to eat sticky chicken until I couldn't possibly eat another bite. I would soon realize what a bad idea that was.

We cleared the table, and AJ's mom took the job of loading the dishwasher. We took the opportunity to disappear. We headed over to HQ to finally talk about all the stuff that had happened earlier that day.

CHAPTER 12

The Curse of the Sticky Chicken

When we got down to HQ, all I wanted to do was lie down on the couch and give my stomach a rest. Scooter went to his computer. AJ went to the fridge, grabbed a pudding cup, and tore it open.

"AJ, how in the world can you still be hungry! I had three helpings, just like you, and I feel like I'm going to explode!" I moaned.

Scooter interrupted without even looking away from his computer. "You ate too much rice, Tyler; it expands in your stomach."

"But it was sooooo good." I moaned, laying as still as I could on the couch. AJ and Scooter just laughed at my misery.

Scooter was the first to get down to business. "Hmm. It looks like the tracker must have fallen off of Jerry's bike. The computer program says the tracker has not moved since earlier today, when Jerry's bike was in Felicia's driveway."

"Oh, great!" I moaned. "Now how are we supposed to figure out where Jerry lives?"

"I think I have a solution to that," Scooter said with a smile.

"Why are we talking about Jerry right now, anyway?" AJ interrupted. "Shouldn't we be talking about what happened earlier in the day? You know, the part about the huge tiger that nearly ate us?"

"And how it seemed to disappear?" I added.

"Yes, that is a head-scratcher," Scooter said. "And it was quite embarrassing that Commander Coleman showed up and we looked like we had made up the whole thing. It's all very perplexing."

"Purple-what?" AJ said.

"Perplexing. It means *confusing*. I don't understand how there could be a tiger chasing us one moment and then gone the next moment, when Commander Coleman goes looking for it."

"Maybe the tiger somehow found a way to escape out of the house," AJ offered. Then he suddenly started looking around, as if the tiger might be lurking behind the couch or something. "Uh, that means the tiger could be on the loose somewhere—anywhere!"

"AJ, I thought you believed all those animals were ghosts," Scooter teased.

"That's true. And that's probably a better explanation of how the tiger disappeared! He could just pass through walls and stuff to avoid being seen by Commander Coleman."

"Oh my goodness, AJ, you are delusional. Do you remember how that tiger crashed open the bathroom door? That tiger was *real*," Scooter argued.

AJ remained silent and frowned. He didn't really have a good explanation for that piece of evidence.

"Maybe the more important question is, how did Jerry escape?" I asked. "Maybe the tiger escaped the same way. I say we focus on finding Jerry, and maybe he can provide some answers."

"Everything seems to keep coming back to Jerry. That's why I was talking about him," Scooter said, shaking his head. "Jerry seems to be the place to get all of our questions answered. We find Jerry; he leads us to A.F. We find Jerry; he leads us to the tiger. We find Jerry; he settles the argument of haunted versus not haunted."

"Haunted!" AJ cast his vote with a smile and a raised hand.

I laughed, "Yeah, let's not leave it up to a vote, AJ."

"Besides," Scooter said, "I think we should be focusing more on the A.F. problem right now."

"We don't really have an A.F. problem anymore, do we?" AJ asked. "Didn't he pretty much say he was done messing with us?"

"And you believe him?" I moaned. Laying on the couch was not really helping my discomfort.

"Yeah, I doubt he is actually done messing with us," Scooter said. "But even if he is, I don't really appreciate being toyed with like we were. Besides, this is the closest we have been to identifying who he is. We now know of someone who has actually met him!"

"We do?" AJ asked, confused.

"Yes! Jerry! Do you remember what Felicia said? Someone approached Jerry about being a junior-level spy for the CIA. Do you really believe such a thing as a junior-level spy exists? And I do not believe it was the CIA Jerry talked to. I think it was A.F."

"Of course!" I said. That was what had been bugging me at Felicia's house. Scooter had just put the pieces together for me: A.F. had sent us chasing after Jerry, but A.F.—not the CIA—had been the one controlling Jerry's movements. So A.F. had been the one to recruit him. That meant that Jerry had actually seen A.F.! "But why?" I asked, "Why would A.F. want to recruit Jerry as a fake spy?"

"That is the part I haven't quite figured out yet. I am hoping that when we catch Jerry it will all make sense."

"Okay-okay-okay! So how are we going to catch Jerry, then," AJ said, impatient as always.

"Certainly not by yelling, 'Hey!' at him the second we see him. That hasn't worked out so well the last few times," Scooter said.

"Sorry, okay? Sometimes I react before my brain kicks in!"

"Yeah, we know," I said, causing all three of us to chuckle.

Scooter started, "So since the tracker is not going to help us find where Jerry lives, or where he might be, I think we need to try and catch him at Felicia's house when he comes to check in on her dog next."

"When will that be?" AJ asked.

"I don't know. We need to figure out when she works next," Scooter answered.

"Yeah, but how do we do that?" I moaned.

Scooter sat thinking for moment. His face lit up. "I have a plan: we get her work to tell us."

Scooter turned around to his computer and quickly ran a search to find the phone number of the diner that Felicia worked at; he remembered their logo from her nametag. When he found the number, he wrote it down on a piece of paper and then held it out for me. "Ty, you want to do this?"

Normally, I would be the one to make a phone call like this, but today I was feeling so bad that I was pretty sure I wouldn't be good at thinking on my feet. And this phone call might require it.

"No, you better do it. I'm not feeling so hot. Just make up a story about being an angry customer… No, better yet, a *happy* customer. You should use the pitch dilator."

"Good idea," Scooter said. He went over to HQ's phone, which sat on a small bookcase. A shoebox sat next to the phone; it was full of various gadgets that had come in handy with past cases. Most of these, Scooter had invented and designed himself. The pitch dilator looked like a kazoo with a dial on top. Scooter had designed it to lower or raise the pitch of songs on the radio. But we had come to discover it was most handy at lowering our voices, so that when we talked on the phone, we sounded like adults instead of kids.

Scooter picked up the phone and dialed the diner. I was impressed with the story he made up. He asked if Fifi was working that night. (He already knew she probably wasn't, since she had worked earlier that day.) When the manager said that no, she had worked earlier in the day, Scooter then asked if she was working the next day. Scooter fed him a line about Fifi being his favorite waitress.

"My wife and I had a hankering for some more peanut-butter pie, and we wanted to make sure Fifi would be there when we come in."

The manager was so proud of the fact that his waitress had left such an impression, that he willingly offered the info that Felicia was working the dinner shift the next day, from 1 till 9 p.m.

Scooter feigned excitement and told the manager that he would come in then, and then he hung up.

"Okay, now that we know when Felicia will be gone at work, what's the plan?" asked the impatient AJ.

"I have an idea, but I am still working out the details in my head—" Scooter began.

My stomach was not feeling any better, so I interrupted, "Hey, guys, my stomach is still really bothering me, so I'm going to head home. I think I will leave the details to you to figure out. Just tell me what time we should meet tomorrow."

"Well, since we know Felicia won't be at work

until one o'clock, we definitely can't do anything before then," Scooter said.

"Okay, that's plenty of time. I will just see you tomorrow, sometime before then." I slowly picked myself off the couch and started hobbling toward the door.

"Okay, see ya, Ty. Sorry you forgot how to eat properly!" AJ laughed as he said goodbye.

Later I would think of plenty of great comebacks, but at the time, I didn't really have the energy to respond with anything other than a weak wave of my hand as I left through the vault door. I had hoped the walk to my house would somehow make my stomach feel better, but I was still hurting when I stumbled in the front door. My parents were sitting on the couch, watching a cooking show with some guy who yells a lot. Ugh, just the thought of food made me feel that much more sick.

My mom could tell something was wrong with me. She jumped up to help. "Honey, what's wrong?"

"Just a stomachache. I think I ate too much dinner."

"What do you mean, 'too much dinner'? Did you eat over there? I thought you were going to miss dinner, and so I made a separate tuna casserole to have ready just for when you got home! I figured you would have quite an appetite by now."

"But, Mom, Mrs. Seeva made us sticky chicken so that we would help her move furniture."

My mom's eyes narrowed. At that moment, I

realized I had said too much. "Tyler, when you asked permission to go over there, you let me believe that you were moving furniture out of the goodness of your heart, not because you were getting paid with sticky chicken. Furthermore, you told me you were going to miss dinner, but you already knew she was going to feed you over there. I cannot believe you lied to me."

When she said that, I had a twinge of pain in my stomach. Even my own body was mad at me. "I didn't lie to you, Mom! I didn't say anything that was not true. You jumped to conclusions, and I didn't stop you."

"You were wrong to do that, and you know it."

"I don't think I was," I groaned. I think deep inside I knew she was right, but I was too proud to give up the argument now.

"Well, how about you march upstairs to your room? You can stay there until you recognize your actions for what they were."

A wimpy "Fine" is all I could muster as I hobbled upstairs to my room. At least there I could stretch out on my bed and give my stomach some much-needed relief. I knew we were going to have a big day the next day, so I just decided to go right to bed. I figured my stomach and my mom's temper would be calmed down by morning, so I tried not to think about anything from the evening. I just wanted to fall asleep. It worked.

Although I would not have thought it possible after how I felt the night before, when I woke up I was starving. I hopped out of bed, and as I reached for my bedroom door, I saw that my mother had taped a note to the doorknob. Mom wrote to tell me she was out running errands, and if I wasn't willing to call her cell and apologize for lying, then I had no business even opening my bedroom door. Apparently, she still felt the same this morning as she did last night. I was still a little ticked off at her overreaction and didn't feel like giving in, so I turned around and crawled back into bed. I laid there thinking about the plan for the afternoon. What would Scooter's plan be for catching Jerry? Would Jerry be able to help us find A.F.? How did Jerry avoid the tiger and escape the house? Somewhere among the questions, I dozed off again.

I don't know what time I had woken up the first time, so I'm not sure how long my little nap was. But when I woke up the second time, it was almost eleven in the morning. I laid there, staring at the ceiling, thinking about what my mom had said the night before. She was wrong, wasn't she? I did not say anything that was not true. So I didn't lie. I wasn't trying to mislead her, or was I? I didn't really know anymore; it's hard to decode what your motives were, after the fact. I wrestled inside for a few more minutes until I could take it no longer. I decided to call my mom.

Now, I admit to you, it wasn't the fact that I

decided I was wrong, or that she was right, or that I was still extremely hungry. It wasn't even the fact that I needed to be able to leave the house later that afternoon. What finally made up my mind for me was the fact that I really had to go to the bathroom! The bathroom was across the hall, and in order to get there, I had to pass by Tamara's room. She had, no doubt, been informed of my situation and would be the first to report my infraction to Mom if I gave her an opportunity.

I noticed that my mom had conveniently left the cordless house phone sitting on my nightstand, so I could call her without leaving my prison. I called her cell phone and prepared for a humbling conversation. I must have caught her in a good mood, though. I jumped right in with the most heartfelt "I'm sorry for lying" speech I could muster. After a little bit of scolding about my taking so long to call her, she forgave me. I think she felt like a night of stomach pain made for a pretty good punishment. I told her that I had some things to do regarding our current case and intended on being home around dinner. She did not plan on being home until around dinnertime, either. We agreed that at dinner, we could talk more about this whole lying issue. If only we would have known then that only one of us would be making that appointment.

CHAPTER 13
The Trap is Set

By the time I got some "breakfast" and got dressed, it was already past noon. I was sort of surprised that I hadn't gotten a harassing phone call from Scooter or AJ. But then again, we did decide we couldn't do anything until after one, when Felicia would be gone for work. I decided to walk and took the shortcut through the woods to go straight to HQ, instead of going down the street to Scooter's house.

When I got inside, it was clear that AJ and Scooter had been there awhile. They had spent a good part of the morning having a rubber band and paper war. For bullets, they had folded up paper into little pellets. They were using rubber bands to shoot the paper at each other. There were now little pieces of paper everywhere! Scooter had pulled the futon cushion off its frame and was using it as a shelter, while AJ was hiding behind the round table, which he had turned on its side. It was clear right away that I needed to pick a side. Of course I picked Scooter's and dove behind the futon cushion he was holding up. It was an easy decision for one huge reason: it meant I had an excuse to shoot at AJ! Scooter and I maneuvered ourselves over to the computer desk so I could get myself a rubber band, and then the three of us shot paper at each other for another thirty or forty minutes.

Well, they say it's all fun and games until someone gets hurt. I'm not sure who *they* are, but in this case, they were right. The game came to a sudden stop when AJ made a perfect shot that nailed Scooter in the ear. Scooter yelped, jumped up, and started hopping around, with his hand covering the side of his head. When he finally moved his hand away, AJ and I could see that Scooter's right ear was bright red.

"That looks like it's going to hurt for a while," I said with a laugh.

"It also looks like I won," AJ said proudly, a huge grin on his face.

"Whatever!" Scooter grumbled as he put his hand back over his right ear.

"Hey, we agreed! Loser has to clean up!" AJ insisted.

I knew AJ was a little bit of a sore winner, so there was no way he was going to clean up, and Scooter was still wincing in pain from his ear. So I decided to just do it myself and avoid any further arguing.

"I'll do it," I said, and I began to pick up all the pieces of paper scattered across the floor. To my surprise, AJ helped me by at least putting the table and couch back the way they belonged.

Once HQ was looking close to normal, I asked, "So, Scoot, what's the plan?"

AJ jumped in, "Oh, it's good, Ty, you're gonna love it!"

"You already went over the plan without me?" I asked Scooter, a little shocked.

"Hey, some of us decided to wake up before noon!" he shot back.

"Okay, you have a point," I admitted. "So fill me in, then."

"I think I will just show you instead. It's after 1. Let's just head down to Felicia's house and get things set up. I have everything we need in my backpack." He pointed at his backpack, which was sitting innocently by the door. "The only thing you guys will need is your radios."

"I have to grab mine from my bedroom, but I have to stop by my house to get my bike, anyway," I said.

"Same for me," AJ said.

"Okay, let's just meet outside Ty's house in ten minutes."

After getting ready and grabbing bikes, we met in my driveway and then took the quick trip down to Felicia's house at the entrance to Hidden Place. We stashed our bikes in the bushes across the street.

The blue sedan was not in the driveway, which

confirmed that Felicia was indeed off at work, like her supervisor had said. Scooter went over to about the spot where Jerry's bike had been sitting the day before. He scanned the pavement for a few seconds and then bent over and picked up what looked like a gum wrapper. It was the lost tracker.

"Yep, I figured that's what happened. It must have fallen off when he climbed onto his bike the last time." He put the tracker in his shorts pocket.

Scooter then went on to explain his plan as he set it up. Scooter figured, since Felicia had probably left a few minutes ago, that we had a couple hours to get ready before we might expect Jerry to show up to check on the pregnant dog, Cici.

Scooter had decided that it was almost impossible to ambush Jerry from the front of the house. There were a couple trees in the front yard, but they were not large enough to hide behind. The nearest good hiding spot was the bushes across the street, where we had put our bikes. It would be hard for all three of us to approach him in the front yard without him seeing us coming. Chances are, he would take off again, and he would have a good head start on us.

Scooter decided to force Jerry to exit from the back of the house, where we had a lot more options. Once Jerry came to the house, he would enter the front door and shut it behind him. AJ would then sneak over to the front door and battery-lock it. Battery-locking is really simple. You just jam two AA batteries in between the door and the door frame, one up near the top and one below at about knee level. The result is, it puts extra pressure on the door so it's impossible to turn the doorknob. It feels like the door is locked, even though it isn't. So after Jerry checked in on the dog, he would try to leave through the front door. The door would not let him out, and eventually he would decide to go out the back door. And the back door is where our trap would be. AJ stayed in the front yard to settle into his hiding spot while Scooter took me around back to set up the next part of the trap.

The back door was the perfect place to lay a trap. The backyard was fairly small and almost completely surrounded by tall trees and thick bushes. We could set up the trap now and not have to worry about it being discovered by Jerry or some nosey neighbor. We wouldn't have been able to set a trap in front because Jerry would see it when he was going into the house.

The back exit from the house was a sliding glass door that exited onto a square wooden deck about ten feet to a side. It was lined with wood railings on two sides, it had the back of the house on the third side, and the fourth side of the deck also had a railing, except for an opening where wooden steps led down about four feet to the ground. Underneath the deck was a lawn mower and an empty trash can. This would make an ideal place for Scooter and me to hide while we waited for Jerry to come out of the house.

Scooter walked up the stairs to the deck. He reached into his pack and pulled out a brown paper bag. He crumpled it up and then uncrumpled it, making quite a few extra wrinkles in it. He did this a few more times until the bag looked like it was going to fall apart.

"I am weakening the bag so it is sure to tear when I want it to, but not before then." He then pulled out a plastic bag of flour and began to empty the flour into the paper bag. As the paper bag filled up, it looked like one accidental poke with a sharp stick would make the thing explode. Scooter tied off the opening of the bag with some string and then hung the bag from the gutter of the roof, just to the left of the sliding glass door. From the deck, it looked sort of like a menacing beehive hanging down from the roof, but from inside the house, Jerry wouldn't even be able to see it.

Scooter then pulled out some fishing line and attached three fishing hooks to one end. He very gently sunk the hooks into the bag of flour. A little flour spilled out in the process, but the bag seemed to be able to handle them. Scooter then took the other end of the line and let it fall to the wooden deck. With a little prodding, the string found a space between the boards of the deck and fell through to the ground below.

Next Scooter took out a small desk fan. I don't know if Scooter was lucky or if he somehow knew it would be there, but there was an electric outlet on the outside of the house. He plugged in the fan and turned it to *Medium*. The fan began to blow with quite a bit of force, and yet it was surprisingly quiet. I guess if a fan like that is usually going to be sitting at someone's desk, it has to be designed that way. He set the fan against the house and pointed it toward the sliding glass door. Once again, someone would not be able to see the fan from inside the house.

Finally, Scooter took one more piece of fishing line and hooked it to the bottom corner of the sliding glass door. He then ran the extra line alongside the house to the edge of the deck. He let the rest of the fishing line fall over the edge.

"Come on," he said without any further explanation. He grabbed his backpack and headed down the stairs. I followed. We then circled behind the stairs and crouched under the deck.

"Please explain," I said.

"Look up," he said. As I looked up, I could see daylight coming from between the boards of the deck. "So after Jerry goes inside, AJ sneaks over and battery-locks the front door. When Jerry realizes something is messed up with the front door, he is going to come out this way. When he steps out onto the deck, I will be able to see him." He pointed at a space directly above where we crouched. "When he is outside, I pull on this string, which rips open the bag of flour. Poof! Jerry is stuck in a white cloud. The fan is to help kick up the flour and make it swirl around longer."

"So what about the other string?" I asked, pointing to the second string, which was hanging over the side of deck.

"That's a safety precaution. When Jerry comes out, as soon as I yank on the flour bag, I need you to pull that string. It should shut the door behind Jerry, cutting off his escape back into the hose and, more importantly, keeping all the flour from floating into Felicia's house." This made him chuckle. "At that point, Jerry should be covered in flour, and the only way for him to leave the deck will be to go down the stairs. But the three of us will be there, blocking his exit."

"Sounds great, Scoot, but what do we do right now?"

"Now, we wait." Scooter leaned against the wall of the house and slowly slid down into a sitting position. He opened his backpack and pulled out his radio and a deck of cards. "You may want to have a seat; this might be awhile."

"What about AJ?" I asked.

"Oh, I am sure he has found a good hiding spot by now." He picked up his radio. "AJ, are you in position?"

"Ten-four," AJ radioed back.

Scooter looked at me, smiled, and put his radio on the ground next to him. He picked up the deck of cards. "So what should we play?"

CHAPTER 14
Shower of Flour

We sat under the back deck playing cards and waiting for at least a couple hours. I felt sorry for AJ. I had Scooter to keep me company, and I was still really bored. I couldn't imagine what it must have been like for AJ to be on solo lookout for that long.

Finally, the radio squawked. It was AJ. "Okay, we have company. Jerry is walking to the front door. Looks like he must have walked from his house; I don't see his bike anywhere in sight."

Scooter and I went on high alert. Scooter reached into his bag and pulled out a pair of thick leather work gloves. He handed me the left, and he slipped on the right. I looked at him, confused. He wrapped the fishing line attached to the flour bag around his gloved hand a bunch of times. I saw now: he was making it possible to hold onto the fishing line without it slipping or cutting into his hand. I followed his lead with the line attached to the back door, wrapping the line around my gloved left hand a bunch of times. Scooter frantically motioned for me to unwrap my line. I was confused; I thought I was supposed to follow his lead.

He finally whispered, "You have to give yourself slack in the line or else Jerry won't be able to get the door open because you are holding it closed!"

Good point, I said to myself. I unraveled about three feet of line so Jerry would be able to slide the door open that far before the door would catch.

The radio crackled again. "Okay, guys, he is not getting out the front door now. And I am back in my hiding spot. I don't think he saw me."

We were now on very high alert. Suddenly, the house started making a loud rumbling noise. Startled, I turned to Scooter and mouthed the words, "What is that?"

Scooter spoke out loud. "I think he must be getting the dog some water. This is an older house, and the pipes are noisy." He wasn't worried about being heard over the thunderous noise that seemed to be coming from the wall we were leaning against.

The howling stopped, and I could feel my heart beating faster and faster in anticipation of what would happen next. A few minutes of near silence followed. Then, as Scooter had predicted, we could hear the sliding glass door open above us. We could see one sole of a shoe step out onto the deck. The other shoe followed. As soon as Scooter saw the second shoe hit the deck above us, he jerked on the fishing line, and we could hear the bag of flour rip open. I couldn't jerk on my fishing line the same way Scooter could; after all, my line was attached to a heavy glass door. Mine was more of a long, steady pull, but the door shut, just as Scooter had planned. We could hear Jerry sputtering with his mouth full of flour. As he stumbled around on the deck, his loud footsteps echoed below. Scooter and I scrambled out from underneath the deck to cover Jerry's one exit, the stairs.

I couldn't help but laugh when I looked up the stairs to what was happening on the deck. Scooter's plan had worked perfectly! All you could see was a huge, white cloud; it looked like the deck was going up in smoke! We could hear Jerry flailing around, but we couldn't really see him through the cloud of flour. Suddenly, there was a big *BAM!* Apparently, Jerry had run smack into the glass door he had just come out of.

Scooter began to worry that Jerry might figure out how to get the back door open and retreat back inside, so he yelled in the deepest voice he could imitate, "Freeze, don't move!"

To our relief and amazement, Jerry obeyed.

About that time, AJ came around the corner and started to ask, "So did—"

Scooter cut him off with a finger to his mouth and then motioned for us to quietly walk up the stairs. We all climbed the stairs, stood at the top of them, and waited. Jerry was still obediently frozen in the midst of the cloud of flour. Scooter pulled the plug on the fan, and the flour began to settle quickly as a result.

I am sure you can imagine the look on Jerry's face when he could finally see through the thinning white mist to see the three of us waiting for him.

Jerry looked at the three of us with a puzzled look. He stared for a minute and then a look of recognition crossed his face. He pointed at us and said, "You..." and that was it. I think he was waiting for us to finish his sentence for him, but we just stood there, silent. Finally, a big smile came across his face. "You guys are with the CIA, aren't you? That's why you've been following me the last few days, huh?"

Scooter decided to play along. "What gave us away?

"Well, I don't see any earpieces in your ears, but I saw your walkie-talkies. Rookie mistake. You guys should really try and keep those more hidden, or you will blow your cover."

"Yes, we will take that under advisement," I said, trying to get in on this little game. "So how is the mission coming? We've been sent to check up on you."

"Wow, you guys are younger than me. How did you guys get junior operative status so quickly?" he asked sincerely. The three of us looked at each other in confusion, not sure what to say. Jerry saw this, and his tone quickly changed. "Hey, wait, I haven't been given a mission for a couple days now. But if you guys were actually with the CIA, you would actually know that! Who are you, really?"

I was about to speak up when Jerry was hit with a realization. "Oh no, my cover has been blown. I've been compromised! Abort!" He turned to run and ran straight into the glass door with a loud *thud*. He staggered backward and fell onto his rear at our feet.

Scooter put his hand on the high schooler's shoulder. It was hard to believe Jerry was bigger and older than all of us. "Calm down. Calm down. We just want to talk. We are actually detectives. We work with the police."

"The police! Hey, I may be a spy, but I have never broken the law while on a mission. Good spies find a way not to."

AJ scoffed and rolled his eyes.

Scooter ignored him and went on. "It's nothing like that. We just have some questions for you about who hired you."

"I can't reveal that; it's classified."

AJ was really getting frustrated with Jerry. "Dude, you are not a spy!"

"Yes, I am!"

"Well, if you are, you're not a very good one," AJ mocked.

"Yes, I am. I have a perfect record of completing missions."

"What kind of a spy gets captured by three teenagers and a bag of flour?" AJ jeered.

This last question seemed to deliver a crushing blow to Jerry. He dropped his head in shame and mumbled, "You are absolutely right. I am a horrible spy. It's a shame to my profession that I would ever get caught, let alone this easily."

I felt sorry for the kid. "Hey, we didn't come here to make you feel bad. We seriously just want to ask a couple questions."

"Fine," said a dejected Jerry.

"Great," I said. "So who hired you?"

Jerry reached into his shorts pocket and pulled out a business card. "His name is Andrew Fenton. He works for the Seattle branch of the CIA." He handed the card to Scooter. The card said exactly what Jerry had just said aloud—nothing more, nothing less.

"Andrew Fenton, huh?" He looked at AJ and me. "Andrew Fenton has the initials A.F." We all gave a knowing nod to each other.

"His initials are A.F. So what?" Jerry asked, confused.

"I'll explain in a minute," Scooter answered excitedly. "Can you describe what A.F., uh, I mean, this *Andrew Fenton* looked like?"

"Very tall, muscular, dark glasses, short black hair in a buzz cut: he looked very secret agent-like to me."

"Oh, so that's what secret agents look like, huh?" AJ said sarcastically.

Scooter told AJ to knock it off and gave him the death stare. He turned his attention back to Jerry. "So what did this guy say to you when he gave you the card and recruited you?"

"And where did he talk to you?" I added.

"He came to my house. I answered the door, and he handed me the card and said, 'Jerry, do you want to serve your country?' I said yes, and then he said, 'Great. We will be in touch.' And then he walked away. It was a very short conversation."

"So how did he 'get in touch' with you later?"

"I got an email from him the next day. I don't know how he got my email address. But he's a spy, so I figured he should know how to get that information."

AJ was even more frustrated now. "For goodness' sakes, A.F. is not a spy, he's a... he's a—" Right then, AJ's phone began singing. As Scooter, Jerry, and I started laughing, he pulled it out of his pocket and answered in frustration without even looking to see who was calling.

"What?! Oh, sorry, Mom!" he said apologetically as he walked down the steps of the deck to have his conversation in private.

I tried to ask a rather useless question while we waited for AJ to finish talking to his mom. "So why do you think this Andrew guy picked you?"

"Well, my whole life I've wanted to be a spy. I've read almost every book there is involving spies. You know the *Secret Agent Andy* comic books? Yeah, I have collected every issue. I even own the rare episode 47, where Dark Dawn thinks he has trapped Andy in the underwater cage, but Andy escapes just in time to stop the bank robbery of the century!

Have you read that one? Oh, sorry if I just spoiled it for you."

AJ finished his conversation and was walking back up the steps as Jerry continued. "Anyway, I have been training to be a spy my whole life. That's why they so aggressively recruited me."

"Oh my, you are so delusional," AJ said to Jerry. He turned to Scooter. "I have to go. My mom just called, and I have to go to some fundraiser thing tonight with my parents. I gotta go get ready. I can tell that this guy is not going to be any help in catching A.F. But, hey, if I'm wrong, call me and let me know what you find out." With that, he hopped down the stairs again and jogged around the corner of the house.

Jerry was the first to speak after AJ was gone. "So what was he talking about? Who is A.F., and why are you trying to catch him?"

Scooter went on to explain to Jerry how we believed that the man that had come to recruit Jerry was actually A.F.—the person we were looking for. Jerry told us that Andrew had given him some fairly easy missions around town, including going to the YMCA everyday to practice "observing human behavior." Scooter then explained how we had been hired by someone who also had the initials A.F., and we were supposed to follow Jerry everywhere he went. And we would know where Jerry was each day because he would be at the Y every day from 10 until noon.

"So as you can see, it can't be a coincidence. One person with the initials A.F. sends you all over town, specifically to the YMCA. Another person with the initials A.F. sends us chasing after you, specifically at the YMCA. It had to be the same person who sent us both on the same wild goose chase."

"Yeah, I guess you're right. Man, I thought I'd finally gotten to be a spy," Jerry said.

"You still might get your chance, Jerry. If A.F. ever contacts you again, we might need your help to catch him."

"Like a double agent? Oh yeah, now you're talking!"

Scooter laughed, "Well, I guess we should help you get cleaned up."

We spent the next several minutes cleaning both the deck and Jerry. The deck was easy to rid of the flour once Jerry told us where to find Felicia's broom, but even after several minutes of work, Jerry was still looking pretty pale from all the flour stuck to his skin, hair, and clothes.

I was pretty bummed. Catching Jerry was supposed to provide a bunch of answers, but it didn't really give us any answers we were looking for. A.F. had all but said in his note that he was done messing with us. We now had a vague description of what he looked like, but that still described a lot of people. Once again, it looked like we were at a dead-end. But then it dawned on me that we could get at least one question answered.

I turned to Jerry. "So I have a question, Jerry. Yesterday, when we were chasing you and you went into the old house at the top of the hill, how did you get out?"

Scooter stopped sweeping the deck and also looked at Jerry, waiting for an answer.

"That falls under classified material. Are you guys sure you have that sort of security clearance?"

"Jerry!" Scooter and I yelled in unison.

"Okay, okay. Just checking," he chuckled to himself and then continued. "Well, that house has been abandoned for years because it is supposedly haunted. Did you know that?"

Scooter gave an exasperated, "Yeah, we know. So what?"

"Well, I never believed it, and I live right next door. So a few years ago, I went inside to try and prove it was not haunted. I figured it would be a good test of my investigative skills and training for future spy missions."

Scooter was growing impatient. "And?"

"And while I was in the house, I stumbled upon a secret."

"What kind of secret?" I asked.

"I think I'll just have to show you. C'mon!" he said as he walked down the stairs of the deck.

"Uh, okay," I said as I followed.

Scooter grabbed his backpack and joined us. When we got to the front of the house, Scooter asked us to hold up for a second. He went over to the front door and pulled out the two batteries that were jammed in between the door and the frame.

"Oh, that must be why I couldn't get the front door to open," marveled Jerry.

"Yeah, we needed to force you out the back door into our trap," I said proudly.

"It worked," Jerry said with a laugh. He shook his hair, and a cloud of white flour drifted away. Jerry went to lock the front door, but Scooter reminded him the back door was also unlocked. Jerry quickly went back through the house to go lock the sliding glass door. He then came out the front and used his key to lock the front door.

As we began walking up the hill, Scooter asked, "So do you think the house is haunted?"

"Me? Nah. I've been in and out of that house hundreds of times and never saw anything I couldn't explain easily enough."

"So then you've never seen a tiger in the house?" I jumped in.

"A tiger? Of course not! That's ridiculous! Just recently, I could have sworn I heard a lion roar or something, but I know my mind is just playing tricks on me. They call that *suggestion*. If you talk about something long enough, your brain starts making it seem real when it isn't." He seemed proud that he had learned that.

It was a good thing that AJ wasn't there; he would have told Jerry about the tiger that we had seen. And based on what Jerry had told us, we would have had another haunted versus not haunted argument on our hands. As it was, Scooter and I just kept the tiger story to ourselves and looked forward to Jerry sharing his secret discovery with us. I had my doubts that this secret would be big enough for me to get excited about—my version of reality was clearly different than Jerry's.

When we got to the top of the hill, Scooter and I instinctively hesitated at the entrance to the Safari House driveway. Jerry did not break stride. He marched right up to the front door without stopping.

Jerry opened the front door and stepped inside, leaving Scooter and me to scramble up the driveway and onto the front porch in order to catch up.

As we went inside the house we saw Jerry over to our left. He was standing in the doorway to the downstairs bathroom.

Walking across the giant hallway, I looked up the giant staircase where we had last seen the tiger. One of the supports to the railing was sticking out to the side. The tiger had probably done that while we were scrambling out the front door. I imagined one swoosh of its tail would probably be powerful enough to knock one of those supports out of place. The thought of such a close call made me shudder.

"C'mon, let's go." Jerry was reminding us he had something to show us. He motioned for us to join him.

As I stepped into the bathroom, I joked, "I'm not sure I want to know what sort of secret you found in the bathroom!"

Jerry was standing near the far wall. "You will want to know about this one," he said, pointing toward a towel rack attached to the wall. It was a silver bar that stuck out from the wall a few inches. It was about two feet wide, and normally you would hang a couple towels on it. But I guessed there had not been a towel hanging there for many many years. Jerry reached out and grabbed the towel bar with both hands. "This is the secret I was telling you about." He then began to lift the bar. I half-expected him to pull the bar off the wall, but instead, an entire section of the wall began to move up with the bar. Hidden behind the section of the wall that had just moved was a tunnel!

"No way!" is all I could say as I stared into the darkness of the tunnel.

"Yes way!" Jerry said proudly. "This tunnel leads to another trap door at the back of the house and empties out into the backyard. The other day when you guys chased me, I crawled into this tunnel, and in no time I was back outside. C'mon, I'll show you."

He quickly crawled head-first into the tunnel, which was about two and a half feet high. Scooter dropped his backpack on the bathroom floor and immediately followed. I crouched down and watched Scooter's legs disappear into the darkness.

I was about to head in myself when suddenly everything went dark. Someone had pulled a huge blanket or something over my head. Strong arms wrapped around me and lifted me into the air. It took me a second to realize that someone had slung me over a shoulder like I was a huge bag of dog food. I should have screamed, but instead I instinctively tried to wrestle with the blanket and the person carrying me. My legs smacked into what must have been the side of the doorway as my kidnapper left the bathroom. It felt like we turned very quickly, and then my head must have smacked the other side of the doorway because I don't remember anything but darkness after that.

CHAPTER 15
Things That Go Bump in the Night

"Tyler? Tyler?"

I could hear Scooter whispering.

"Tyler, are you in here?"

It was dark, and my head was hurting like crazy. It was hard to breathe. I realized my head was underneath a blanket of some sort. My head was throbbing, and I let out a slow moan.

"Tyler? Is that you?" Scooter's voice asked me again.

"Yeah, it's me," I groaned. "Uh, where am I?"

"I don't know; we can't see. We're kind of stuck over here."

"We?" My head was spinning. What was Scooter talking about? "AJ, are you stuck too?"

"No, it's me and Jerry."

"Jerry?" I asked, trying to figure out what was the last thing I remembered.

"Yes, Jerry. Remember, he was showing us his

secret tunnel? Someone kidnapped us. We've been stuck in these sheets for hours now. You must have been asleep because you have been quiet the whole time. We thought they took you somewhere else until I heard you groaning just then."

Kidnapped? Really? Caught in sheets? I started to remember a sheet being pulled over my head. *Oh, that's right! Then someone picked me up, and then—* bam—*I hit my head!* My head started to throb even more as I recalled more details. "Oh yeah, I'm starting to remember."

"Well, can you see anything? Do you have any clue where we are? Jerry and I are somehow tied up and can't see a thing. We are pretty stuck; we have been trying for some time, and we are not getting out."

I tried to pull the blanket off of me and couldn't seem to get it to move. I was lying on my back, and the blanket seemed to be tucked underneath me. I rolled over onto my stomach, and then the blanket still seemed to be tucked underneath me. This probably wouldn't have been so hard if my head wasn't in such a fog, or if it wasn't so dark. I got up on my hands and knees, and the blanket seemed to be pulling me down. In frustration, I stopped and just took a deep breath.

That's when I finally figured out that I was not under a blanket at all. I was in some sort of cloth sack. This triggered a memory of earlier, when I had been grabbed. Someone had slipped this sack over my head and had pulled it all the way down over my whole body—my whole body except for my feet! I remembered that my feet were outside the bag because I had been kicking them around when I smacked into the doorway. I tried to move my feet and realized they were free. The bag seemed to have been pulled down to about my shins. As quickly as I could, I started to wiggle my way backward out of the bag. My arms were now free, and I reached up and pulled the sack the rest of the way off of my head.

Freedom! I took a big gasp of cooler air. I had thought the inside of the bag wasn't the most pleasant smell, but it was wonderful compared to the smell of whatever room I was in. It smelled like we were at the horse stables at the county fair. I am sure you know what kind of smell I'm talking about! I was in a dark room, not quite pitch black, but pretty close.

I was still trying to take in my surroundings when Scooter hollered, "Tyler, are you still there? Are you stuck or what?"

"No, I just got free," I answered.

"Then get us out of here!"

I could tell by his voice that Scooter was only a few feet away from me. I crawled toward him and bumped into him with my forehead. I winced in pain. Just bumping my head was enough to make it throb again.

"Ow!" he whined as well.

I fumbled around with the cloth wrapped around Scooter. It became clear very quickly that he had been stuffed into a similar bag, but in Scooter's case, they had gotten his entire body inside, cinched the bag closed, and tied the bag off in a series of crazy knots. It took me several minutes to untie all the knots. Between the darkness, my head still feeling fuzzy, and Scooter's constant squirming, it probably took a lot longer than it should have.

Once Scooter was free, he ripped the bag off his head and sucked in a huge breath of what he thought would be fresh air. "Aaaak" is all he could manage to say, as he gagged on the putrid smell.

I fumbled with my hands until I found Jerry. He was tied up in a bag just like Scooter had been. Jerry was not moving at all. "Uh, Scoot, Jerry is not moving!" I said in a panic.

"It's okay. When we first got here, Jerry was having a panic attack from being stuck in his sack. I think he is claustrophobic. I think he is just sleeping."

As if on cue, Jerry started to stir. The second he felt me touching the knots of his bag, he started thrashing about.

"Jerry! Stop moving. This is Tyler. I am working on getting you out of there."

"Okay, okay," he said, and he settled down.

After working on Scooter's knots, I felt like I was an expert, and it took a lot less time to get Jerry out.

He scrambled out of his sack, and before even looking around, he yelled, "We're saved!"

"Not exactly," Scooter grumbled.

"Huh?" said Jerry, followed by an "Ugh!" as he caught a whiff of whatever that smell was.

"I was wondering what this thing was sticking into my back, and I think it is a metal bar. I think we are in some sort of cage," Scooter said.

We all reached out and moved around until we found the bars surrounding us. We were indeed in a cage. I couldn't tell, but I was guessing the size of the cage was about eight feet on each side.

Jerry spoke up, "Hey, guys, I think I found the door! but it feels like it's locked. I think there's a lock on the outside."

Scooter went over to feel what Jerry was talking about. He confirmed that it was a lock that would require a key. He banged the lock against the cage in frustration. The metal on metal made a loud noise that echoed around the room. It also hurt my already throbbing head. Just then, I thought I heard a low growl from somewhere across the room.

"Did you hear that?" I asked.

"Yeah, it sounded like a—" Jerry's comments were cut off by an even louder growl. I was pretty sure I recognized that noise: there was a tiger in the room, and it did not sound happy!

"Quickly, everyone to the center of the cage," Scooter instructed.

Jerry and I did our best in the dark to find what we thought was about the middle of the cage. We then turned, and all three of us leaned our backs against each other to face outward. It would have been much more comfortable to stretch my legs out in front of me, but I had them pulled in close to my body to keep every part of me as far away from the edge of the cage as possible. I assumed Scooter and Jerry were doing the same thing.

Apparently, the tiger had awakened in a bad mood and he believed it was our fault, because he spent the next five minutes snarling and hissing at us. Every move he made echoed throughout the room, so it was hard to tell exactly where he was, which made it that much more unnerving. Not that I've had a lot of experience in this sort of thing, but I have never been happier to be locked in a cage!

As we began to feel a little bit safer huddled in the middle of the cage, Jerry tried to lighten the mood with a joke: "Well, the good news is, we don't have to wonder where that smell is coming from anymore." All three of us laughed uncomfortably.

After about ten minutes, the tiger calmed down. "Maybe it is going to sleep," Scooter whispered. "I think that might be a good idea for all of us."

"Okay," whispered Jerry.

I didn't say anything, and they probably thought that I agreed that it was a good idea. But really, I thought it was a terrible idea. The last thing I was going to do was sleep. What if I dozed off, and in my sleep I rolled over so an arm or leg was near the edge of the cage?

So while the others, I assumed, were trying to get

some rest, I sat as still as possible and used every trick I could think of to try and stay awake. I thought about the case; I thought about my dad, my mom, my sister; I tried tapping my fingers quietly on my leg. It seemed no matter what I did to stay awake, it just made me more sleepy. I had no clue what time it was, but I was pretty sure it wasn't so late that I shouldn't be able to stay awake. I fought the urge to close my eyes, but it was so boring to stare at darkness with them open that I closed them just to give them a rest. That was a mistake because it was only a few minutes later that I was fast asleep.

CHAPTER 16
Hurry Up and Wait

The next morning (at least I assume that it was morning) I was awakened by Scooter nudging me.

"Ty, wake up. We need your help."

I opened my eyes, and as my eyes adjusted to the morning light, the cage bars came into focus. I remembered something the previous night about bars, a cage, a tiger… A tiger! I bolted up into a sitting position, eyes wide open, looking around. "Where's the tiger?"

Scooter laughed, "Don't worry. He is not going to get us. Look." He pointed across the room.

As I took in the rest of the room, I could see what was so funny. Jerry, Scooter, and I were in a cage on one side of a very large room, and there was indeed a tiger in the room with us. But the tiger was safely in its own cage on the other side of the room. Apparently, between the dark and the echoes, the tiger had sounded like it was only feet away! As I laughed to myself, I looked around the rest of the room; there was not much to look at. There was a third cage, but it was empty. All three cages were of similar design: a thin sheet of metal for the top and the bottom, with thick metal bars running up and down on all four sides. The bars were about four inches apart.

We must have been in some sort of basement because the ceiling was much lower than a normal room, and we could see the wood supports of the floor above us. There were two small windows up near the ceiling. The windows were covered with cardboard, but a little bit of light was streaming in around the edges of the cardboard. In the corner of the room, there were some stairs which led up and out of view.

"Ty, are you going to help or not?" Scooter said. He and Jerry were standing above me impatiently.

"Uh, yeah, sorry. What's up?" I said as I got to my feet and then bent over a little. The cage we were in was six feet tall, so none of us had to duck, but with the roof of the cage that close, I found myself bending over a little anyway.

"Okay, see that window over there?" He pointed at one of the two windows across the room. "We need to get over to find out if we can see anything and then figure out where we are."

"That is like ten feet away. How do you expect us to do that?" I asked.

"I am glad you asked. I was looking at this cage, and it reminded me of a story," Scooter began. He loved telling stories. "Do you remember when Urpy kept getting out of his crib, and we could never figure out how?"

"Yeah, I remember," I said. Urpy is Scooter's three-year-old brother. His real name is Wyatt, but we nicknamed him Urpy. If you want to know why, read the previous case files.

"Well, my parents finally figured it out one night when they caught him in the act. Basically, he was shaking his crib so much that it would wobble across his bedroom floor. Once he got it over to the other side of the room, there was a dresser that he could climb onto and get down from there. He would then push his crib back into place as if nothing had ever happened."

"And then he would wander into the living room and ask your mom for a 'sammich' as if nothing was wrong!" I added with a laugh.

"Smart kid," Jerry marveled.

"Well, I think we can do the same thing here." Scooter said. "This cage is much bigger than a crib, but the three of us together weigh a lot more than Urpy. Plus, it looks like this cage was built to be pretty light, so we have that going for us too."

"So how do you suppose we do this?" I asked.

"I think we all line up on one end of the cage, we run over together and slam into the far side of the cage, and it should slide across the floor, slowly but surely."

"It's worth a try," Jerry said encouragingly.

"Nothing to lose," I added.

We lined up on the far side of the cage, and on Scooter's count of three, we ran over and threw our weight into the wall of bars on the far side. As the cage rubbed against the floor, it made the loudest, most irritating screech I have ever heard. Imagine someone rubbing two pieces of Styrofoam together, but over the intercom at school! The hairs on the back of my neck stood up in protest. All three of us instinctively put our hands over our ears. I looked over at the tiger in the other cage. The loud noise had aroused him from his nap, and he quietly paced in his cage, watching our commotion.

Scooter offered a positive spin on things. "Well, with this much noise, maybe someone will hear us!"

"Yeah, hopefully it won't be whoever put us down here," I said.

Scooter walked over to the other side of the cage and looked down. "Hey, it worked! We moved about six inches!"

I went over to see what he was talking about. As I looked down, I could see a little rust line where the cage used to be just a minute ago. I started to do some mental calculations. Scooter's idea was working, but it was going to take a whole bunch more times. I wasn't sure my ears were going to be able to handle it.

"Well, let's do it again," I said with limited enthusiasm.

We lined up and did the same thing again, but

fortunately, this time it made not nearly as much noise as the first time. We went over to look at how far the cage had moved, and we found it had moved quite a bit more than the first time as well. Apparently, the cage had just been in the same spot for way too long, and once it started moving, it was good to go.

I lost count of how many times we crashed into those bars in order to get across the room, but fortunately, it was a lot less than I thought it would be. Still, I think we were all pretty sore and glad to be done with it. The cage was now only about two feet away from the wall where the window was. Scooter reached up and grabbed the piece of cardboard that was blocking the small window. As he pulled it away, bright light came flooding into the room, and we all shielded our eyes because we were used to the darker room.

After his eyes adjusted, Scooter looked out the window. "Unfortunately, from this angle all you can see is blue sky. That is not going to help us figure out where we are. So let's just go with what we know."

"What do we know?" Jerry asked.

"Well, we know we are in a basement," I began. "The only times I have ever seen small windows like this up near the ceiling, were in basements. And this basement is probably almost all below ground. That window is probably right at ground level."

"And we know we can't be very far from the Safari House," Scooter said. "It didn't seem like it took very long from when they caught us to when they put us in this cage."

"Hey, speaking of which, how did they catch you? The last I saw of you before I was taken you were headed down the tunnel." I said.

"Well," Jerry explained, "when we got farther into the tunnel, we realized you weren't following. Scooter called back to you, but you didn't answer. We decided to go back and find out what was up, so we just backed our way to the bathroom."

"It's really hard to turn around in there," Scooter added. "Anyway, the second we got back into the bathroom, they grabbed us and put us in those bags." He pointed at the cloth bags we had wrestled our way out of the night before. They looked like the sort of bag that you put dirty laundry in at a hotel.

"So how many guys were there? Did you get a good look at them?" I asked.

"I actually didn't see a thing," Scooter said. "The second I got out of the tunnel, they had that bag over my head."

Jerry said, "He shouted, so I stopped backing up, but then someone grabbed me, pulled me out backwards, and bagged me too."

Scooter said, "It sounded like only two of them, one to grab each of us. I didn't hear you, so it's possible that a third person had taken you away already, or you might have just been unconscious in the room."

"Hmm, so maybe two, maybe more. Okay. Sorry, I just never got a chance to ask last night."

"No prob," Scooter said. "It doesn't look like we are going to be any closer to finding out where we are based on the clues we have, anyway." He slumped down, sat with his back against the cage, and put on his thinking face.

I looked up at the window. Scooter was right: all you could see was blue sky and, of course, the sun. "Man, that sun is bright." I turned away.

Suddenly, Scooter jumped up. "You're right, Ty! That sun is bright." He started looking around the room for something that he failed to explain to Jerry or me.

"What are you looking for?" I asked.

"I am looking for something shiny—something like that!" He pointed at the third cage, the one that was empty. Inside the cage was a metal bowl, probably used to hold water or food for whatever animal used to be caged there.

"You want the bowl?" I asked in disbelief.

"Yes, if I can hold that up here to the light, the sun will reflect off of it and create a glare through the window. I am hoping that someone will see that and come over for a closer look."

"That sounds like really wishful thinking," I said.

"If you have a better idea, I am all ears," Scooter countered.

"Not really."

"Then let's figure out how to get that bowl," he said.

The empty cage containing the bowl was about four feet away. The bowl was small enough that if we could get it to tip over on its side, it would be able to fit through the bars of the cage.

"I have an idea," Jerry said proudly, happy to be contributing. He took off his belt and held on to the buckle. He then reached through the bars of our cage and swung the belt towards the metal bowl in the other cage. He hit the bowl on the first try. Unfortunately, the belt was not heavy enough to cause the bowl to move an inch.

Jerry pulled the belt back in and sat down, dejected. "It was worth a try."

"Actually, I think you were onto something," Scooter said. He began to untie his shoe. "You just need some more weight."

Scooter took his shoe off and then grabbed the belt from Jerry. Using the shoelaces, he tied the shoe to the buckle end of the belt and then went over to try the same thing Jerry had. Scooter didn't have Jerry's aim, but on the third try, he got his shoe to land right in the middle of the bowl! He slowly pulled, and the bowl slid over to the bars of the cage and got stuck. Sitting on its base, the bowl was almost twice as wide as the opening between the bars. We were going to have to get the bowl to turn on its side in order to get it out of the cage. About this time, I realized that if we really wanted to, we could just crash into the side of our cage again and slowly move it near the other cage. But I decided not to mention it because I wasn't sure my shoulders could withstand any more. Besides, this was sort of fun, and we had nothing better to do.

Scooter pulled the shoe out of the bowl and brought it back into our cage. He handed the contraption to Jerry. "Okay, Jerry, I need your good aim. I need you to land the shoe on the side of the bowl and get the bowl to stand on its side."

Jerry stood up and once again hit exactly what he was aiming for on the first try. The shoe went between the bars and hit the side of the bowl. But Scooter probably did not anticipate what happened next. The bowl shot straight up in the air and did a few flips on the way back down. It landed upside down and partially on the shoe. This wasn't what we intended, but it looked like it would work out fine, anyway. Jerry was now able to slowly lift the shoe, which in turn lifted one side of the bowl until it was almost resting on its rim. Jerry then slowly pulled the shoe toward him, and the bowl came with it, sliding between the bars of the cage and clanging on the floor once it was free. The bowl was now close enough for Scooter to reach his arm out, grab it off the floor, and bring it into our cage.

"Nicely done, Jerry," I said.

Jerry was beaming. "Thanks."

Scooter took the bowl and went back over to the window. At first he held the bowl at such an angle that the sun's reflection hit me in the face, and I was temporarily blinded.

"See, it's bright! If anyone walks near wherever we are, they should have no problem seeing this." He held the bowl up, and we saw the reflected spot of light hit the window. Then he started turning it back and forth so the spot moved around in the window. "If I do this, there is a better chance people will see it. Movement catches people's eyes."

"So how long are you going to stand there and wave that thing?" I asked jokingly.

"Until I get tired. And then it will be your turn," Scooter laughed.

Well, I guess that's what I get for being a smart-aleck, I said to myself.

Scooter stood and held the bowl in front of the window, while Jerry and I balled up the cloth sacks we had been captured in and used them as padding as we sat and leaned our backs against the bars of the cage. We took turns telling stories and making up riddles for each other to solve. Every few minutes we would trade off, and someone else would take his turn waving the bowl in front of the window while the other two would rest.

I was hungry. I was thirsty. I hadn't eaten in over a day. I had to use the bathroom. My head still hurt from knocking into the door frame. My whole body hurt from repeatedly hurling myself against the bars of the cage in order to move it. And now my arms were tired from holding a stupid bowl in the sunlight. I began to moan and whine every time it became my turn to stand and hold the bowl above my head. I'm sure the others were feeling the same way. Our turns grew shorter and shorter, which meant we had to get up more often. After a couple hours, I think we were all about ready to give up.

Finally, something happened. It was during a shift change. Scooter's arms had gotten tired, and so he had asked me to take over. As he handed me the bowl, the room suddenly got dark. There was a loud knocking coming from outside. I looked up at the window, and who would be blocking the window but AJ!

CHAPTER 17
Freedom!

"AJ, we're here!" Scooter yelled, as if he was worried AJ would walk away if he didn't hear us.

AJ's reply was muffled because of the window in between. "Yeah, I can see you. I have Commander Coleman and the police with me." AJ turned away and said something that we couldn't make out to someone that we couldn't see. He then started pointing toward the little window and nodding his head. I assumed he was talking to Commander Coleman. He turned back to the window.

"Why are the police with you?" Scooter asked.

"Dude, no one had any clue where you were for almost an entire day," AJ said with a laugh. "You should be glad the whole Army isn't looking for you. Your moms would have called them if they could."

"So where are we, anyway?" Scooter yelled, looking up at AJ in the window. "And how did you find us?"

"You don't know?" AJ asked. "You're in the basement of the old Safari House."

"What? I didn't even know the Safari House had a basement!" I yelled.

"I know; neither did I! The police just went inside to find the door to the basement."

As if on cue we started to hear heavy footsteps on the ceiling above us. AJ took a moment to look around the room from his little window. "Dude, are you guys in a cage? How in the world did you end up in there?"

"It's a long story; can we talk about it once you get us out of here?" Scooter yelled in frustration. For some reason, at that moment the tiger decided Scooter was too loud and snarled. All three of us jumped back out of reflex.

AJ saw us and asked, "What is it? Do you see something?"

"Oh, it's just the tiger," I said casually, now realizing that AJ couldn't see that the tiger was in its own cage.

"What?!" AJ started freaking out. We all tried to hide our laughter.

Scooter joined in on the fun. "Don't worry, Aidge, we are safe as long as we stay in this cage. But I would be careful if I were you when you come down here. Whoa!" He jumped in fake fear as if the tiger was taking a swipe at him from nearby.

"Oh my goodness! Okay, I will tell the cops to hurry!" AJ yelled. He got up and ran away from the window. The three of us busted up laughing. After our emotional night, we needed a good laugh.

We could hear many sets of footprints marching around upstairs, and I began to wonder what was taking them so long to come and get us out of this cage.

After a few minutes, AJ reappeared at the window, "Hey, guys, there must be some sort of hidden stairs down to the basement. The police have looked everywhere and can't figure out how to get down to where you are."

Scooter put on his thinking face, but it was Jerry who spoke up. "I'm guessing there's a secret passage to the basement. We already know of one secret passage; why couldn't there be more?"

"A secret passage? How cool!"

Jerry yelled, "Tell them to look for any bars or handles that they can slide a different direction than you normally would." He was probably thinking this secret passage could have a similar door to the one in the bathroom.

AJ yelled back through the window, "But how are we going to know where to look?"

"Give me a sec to think," Scooter said as he held up a finger to AJ. After a moment he asked, "So where is this window that you are looking in? Is it in the front of the house? The back? One of the sides?"

"Uh, this window is in the front. On the opposite side of the front porch from the driveway," AJ answered.

"Okay, I have to think about this..." Scooter trailed off. He turned away from the window and started to think out loud while pointing various directions. "So if the stairs leading down are over there, and the front of the house is there, and the entryway would be there..." His words trailed off again as he continued to think. We all just stared at him, watching the wheels turn in that big brain of his. Suddenly, he snapped out of it. He yelled at AJ, "According to my calculations, the stairs to the basement should be near the kitchen."

"Okay," yelled AJ, and he took off again.

After he was gone, I started thinking a little bit more about it. I figured Scooter thought the entrance had to be near the kitchen because the stairs we could see in the basement were probably directly below the kitchen, but something I remembered seeing the day before made me think the hidden passage to the basement didn't begin there. Unfortunately, I couldn't quite figure out what that something was.

AJ was back in a minute. He was starting to get panicky. "They can't find any handles or anything in the kitchen. They are about to start busting into walls and stuff."

"No, wait," I yelled at AJ. Something about the word *handles* helped me place that thing that was bothering me. "First, go check the big staircase that leads to upstairs. Stand on the right side of the stairs, and try pulling each of the bars underneath the railing toward you."

"What? Why?" AJ asked in hurried frustration.

"I think that bar is what you're looking for," I said.

"Okaaaaay," AJ said, with clear doubt in his voice. He took off from the window again.

I turned away from the window to find Jerry and Scooter giving me confused looks. I explained, "When we were upstairs yesterday and Jerry was taking us to the bathroom secret passage, I remember noticing one of those bars from the railing. It was sticking out to the side as if it was broken. I remember thinking that maybe the tiger did it, but now I'm thinking it's probably the handle to the secret door they're looking for."

"Interesting" is all Scooter could say.

I found myself holding my breath as I waited for either a bunch of police officers to come running down the stairs into the basement or AJ to reappear at the window to tell me I was crazy. Well, neither of those things happened exactly.

There was a loud creak that could be heard from up the stairs. The tiger jumped up and started pacing back and forth in his cage. This was a good sign; he had probably heard that same creak many times before—right before someone brought him food.

"Boys, are you all right?" a familiar voice said from somewhere up above. It was Commander Coleman.

"Yeah, come on down," a very happy Scooter yelled back.

"Uh, what about the tiger?" Coleman asked.

We all laughed. We had forgotten about our little joke on AJ.

Scooter spoke up, "It's okay. He is actually in his own cage. You might want to bring him some sort of snack, though; he looks pretty hungry. And you are going to need some sort of tool to cut the lock off our cage. We are locked in."

Three seconds later we could see a pair of boots descending the stairs. "Actually, I don't think that will be necessary." It was Commander Coleman, and he was jingling a ring of keys. He looked over at the tiger, which was pacing even faster now. "Whoa! That is a BIG kitty." He smiled, walked over to the side of our cage, and started trying to fit a key into the lock.

"Wh-where did you..." Scooter stuttered as he pointed at the keys.

"Oh, these were actually hanging on a hook right at the top of the stairs. When you said you were locked in, I knew exactly what these were for." He smiled. For some reason I could not breathe that sigh of relief until that exact moment I saw him smile.

CHAPTER 18
Post-Apocalypse Pizza

Coleman eventually got the door open, and the three of us gave him a quick thank-you hug and then scrambled up the stairs. At the top of the stairs, we had to turn a corner and then head down a hallway, which, sure enough, spit us out underneath the main staircase in the entryway. The secret entrance was a section of the wall that swung open just like a door, and sure enough, a bar underneath the railing worked as a lever to make that section of the wall open. Both sides of the movable section of wall had the same dark red wallpaper, so even with the door open, it blended in with the surrounding walls.

I didn't really stop to give it a more thorough look because I had three things I needed to take care of, and now that my adrenaline had all worn off, I was very aware of all three. I had not used a bathroom in almost an entire day, and it had been that long since I had eaten as well. But probably the most urgent thing was some fresh air. I had spent way too long in that gross basement to want anything else more. I hurried for the front door. Apparently, Scooter and Jerry felt the same way because we were literally racing each other to see who could get outside first.

We piled out onto the front porch, and as we hung over the railing, we took in some refreshing deep breaths. It felt so nice to finally breathe fresh air that I temporarily forgot how much I needed the bathroom.

Commander Coleman came out a minute later. He told us that he had just called my mom and she was going to come pick up Scooter, AJ, and me. He had not talked to Jerry's parents yet and needed a phone number. Jerry told him not to bother; he lived practically next door and would just walk home. Coleman insisted that he still needed that phone number, and so Jerry sighed and gave it to him. I noticed that for some reason, Scooter was trying to memorize it. I could see his lips moving as he repeated the number over and over under his breath.

Commander Coleman then wanted to hear everything we could remember regarding how we had gotten stuck down in the basement in the first place. He wanted to know everything we could remember about the man or men who had grabbed us. Unfortunately, we didn't see anything and didn't have a lot to give him. We did tell him about the bathroom secret tunnel and how we figured out where the tunnel to get downstairs was. He complimented us on our detective work and then apologized to us for not believing our story about the tiger when we had called 911 a couple days before.

"I don't know how you guys seem to find yourselves in the middle of such unbelievable situations, but from now on, no matter how bizarre, I will believe you if you claim something is possible," he said with a smile. "Now, I need to talk to my guys inside and see if they found anything else useful." He turned and walked back in the front door.

Right on time, I saw a familiar car drive up the hill and pull into a makeshift parking spot short of where the hedge began alongside the driveway. It was my parents. My mom almost got out of the car before it stopped. She moved between two police cars and then cut across the yard as best she could through the tall grass.

"Tyler, I am so glad you're alright! We were so worried about you."

"Sorry I missed our dinner reservation," I joked. It was the only thing I could say without breaking down.

"You are forgiven," she joked back. "I knew you were in trouble when AJ didn't even know where you were."

"So how did he find us, then?" Scooter wondered.

"I don't really know. You will have to ask him," she answered. "All I know is, I was pretty upset when Tyler didn't show up for dinner last night like he promised. When it got to be 8 and you still had not come home or even called, I was no longer mad but worried. I called Mrs. Parks, and she hadn't heard from Scooter, either. Then I called AJ's mother, and she said that AJ was with her. I was so confused; usually you three boys stick together—"

She stopped in mid-sentence. She turned to Jerry, who had just been observing the whole conversation. She reached out her hand. "Hi, you must be Jerry."

"Yes, ma'am," he said politely.

"The last place AJ had seen these two boys was when they were talking to you. So we thought maybe you guys were goofing off at your house. But we didn't know where that is. Obviously, that's not where you boys were." She let out an uncomfortable laugh. "Well. I am sure your parents are worried sick about you. You need to head home and let them know you're safe. Can I give you a ride?"

"No, thank you. I actually live right next door to this place." He pointed at a house just down the hill. He hopped off the railing he had been sitting on and walked down the porch steps. "Nice to meet you. Sorry it had to be like this." He started jogging down the driveway toward his house.

"So when did AJ finally figure out where we were?" I said.

"Well, last night he had no clue, but then today around lunchtime, he called and said he had a new hunch. He was going to call his friend Commander Coleman with the police and see if the Commander could help him find you. Obviously, he was right."

"It looks like AJ is not as useless as we once thought," Scooter joked. The two of us laughed pretty hard. My mom tried to act like that comment was uncalled for, but we could see she was trying hard not to chuckle as well. The front door opened, and out walked AJ. We abruptly stopped laughing.

AJ looked around, wondering what was suddenly not so funny, but then he shrugged it off and announced, "So Commander Coleman says they have a lot of stuff they need to process. He says we should all go to one of our houses and wait for him to come talk to us there."

My mom jumped in, "I think that is an excellent idea, AJ. Boys, I am guessing you're starving, aren't you? Let's go to my house, and I can fix you guys some sticky chicken."

"Ugggh," I moaned. Even after not eating for a whole day, the last thing I wanted to eat was sticky chicken.

"I'm just kidding, dear. We already ordered pizza on the way over."

Look at Mom, thinking she's funny, I said to myself.

My mom went on, "AJ and Scooter, your parents can meet us there."

We all piled into the car and waited for my dad to finish talking with one of the officers. Since my mom had made a beeline for us on the porch, my dad had gotten out and gone over to get the scoop from a police officer who was filling out paperwork in the driveway.

When my dad got into the driver's seat, he turned around to face me. He looked right into my eyes and said, "I am so glad to see you are okay, Son." He turned back around to start the car. He then joked, "Well, AJ, since we found Tyler, I guess I need you to give back all his baseball cards that I gave you." This earned him a weak slap on the shoulder from my mom, as if to say she didn't find his humor funny.

On the short drive home, Mom managed to call both Scooter's and AJ's parents and tell them that all three boys were safe and sound and that they should come over to my house. There, we could all catch up while we waited for Commander Coleman to share what he had learned.

Since AJ and Scooter lived so close to me, by the time we pulled in the driveway, AJ's parents were walking up, and Scooter's mom, dad, and brother were parked on the street, waiting for us. Hugs and kisses were passed around until my mom reminded everyone that neither Scooter nor I had eaten since sometime the day before. She invited everyone inside to make themselves comfortable.

As soon as we got inside, though, every adult began to pepper us with questions all at the same time. Some, we knew the answers to, but most, we didn't, or at least had not had time to figure them out yet. At one point the overwhelming need to use the bathroom came flooding back, and I used it as good excuse to take a break from the questions and rush to the upstairs bathroom. Unfortunately, when I came back, the adults picked right up where they had left off and just asked more questions.

Finally, the doorbell rang, and my mom announced that pizza was here. To our relief, my dad suggested the adults give us boys a chance to put food in our mouths and not have to answer questions for a little bit. The adults decided to go enjoy their coffee in the living room and leave us kids alone in the kitchen to feast. After inhaling the first couple pieces of pizza, Scooter and I finally felt like talking with AJ. He had not missed three meals like us, but he still managed to find a way to scarf down some pizza right alongside us.

Scooter spoke up first. "So, AJ, I am just curious how you were able to find us."

AJ put his half-eaten slice of pizza down and then lowered his voice as he began. "So I really had no clue where you guys went after I left. When Tyler's mom called asking where you were, I could honestly tell her I didn't know. I thought maybe you guys went over to Jerry's house and lost track of time or something. Anyway, this morning when I still had not heard from you, I thought maybe you had left me a message down in HQ or something. So I went over there to see if you had. Nothing."

AJ paused, his eyes got really big, and a huge grin came across his face. He was really proud of this next part. "So then I had a funny thought: 'Man, it sure would have been nice if I had put one of those trackers on you guys.' But then I thought, 'Nah,' because we already saw the one tracker fall off Jerry's bike. But then I remembered that Scooter had picked up Jerry's lost tracker and had stuck it in his pocket."

At this moment, things clicked for Scooter. He reached into his pocket and pulled out the tracker he had picked up the day before from Felicia's driveway.

Scooter interrupted AJ's thought. "You were able to track us because I had this in my pocket, weren't you?"

"Yeah, luckily you still had the tracking software up on your computer in HQ. It showed that the tracker was up near the top of the hill of Hidden Place, so I guessed you must be at the old Safari House. I called Commander Coleman, and we headed up there. I wasn't sure where to look until I saw something shiny out of the corner of my eye. It was a reflection in that window that I found you guys in. I would have never thought that the old Safari House had a basement."

Scooter elbowed me. "See, I told you that bowl would save us!"

"What do you mean?" AJ asked.

"Never mind. It's an inside joke," Scooter said.

"Whatever," AJ responded, stuffing his face with pizza to mask his confusion.

About that time, we heard a commotion in the living room. Commander Coleman had just arrived.

We each grabbed our plates of pizza and brought them into the living room to hear what he had to say.

Coleman remained standing near the front door, where my dad had just let him in. The other parents were sitting on the couches in the living room, and Scooter, AJ, and I stood near the kitchen doorway, holding our plates of pizza.

Coleman explained that the tiger that was locked up in the basement, they believed to be a near-extinct Siberian Tiger. They had a local zoo coming to confirm and probably take custody of it. There was evidence that other animals had been kept down in the basement, but they were not sure what kind. There was no sign of the guys who had taken us and locked us down there. The police had a couple of theories of what the kidnappers were up to, but it was going to take a couple more days to go through the house and look for any more evidence. No one had any idea where they might be now.

"I have a good idea of what they were up to," Scooter jumped in. "As Mr. Pate has explained to us boys before, there are many people who think that house is haunted by ghosts of wild animals or something."

Coleman raised an eyebrow at the interruption. You could tell he was used to working with cold, hard facts and not ghost stories.

"Wait, hold on. Hear me out," Scooter begged. "I think that the kidnappers have heard of these stories too, and I think that they were smuggling animals in that house."

"Really?" my mom chimed in.

"Yes," he answered her and then turned back to Coleman. "That tiger is really rare, right? Almost extinct?"

"Yes, at least that is what the guy from the zoo thinks."

"So I am guessing that tiger would probably sell for a lot of money. And what better place to keep a tiger then a place that has a reputation for haunted animals making noises at all times of day?"

Commander Coleman was impressed. "That is one of the better theories we've been working with, Scooter, though it is mostly conjecture at this point. I'm waiting to hear back from some of my people who are searching for anyone trying to buy or sell rare animals."

He turned to our parents sitting on the couches. "Well, it is still early in our investigation, so that is all we know at this point." He turned to the three of us boys. "So for the next few days, we need you guys to stay away from that house, okay?"

My mom jumped in before we could answer. "Oh, don't worry. They will have no problem staying *far* away from that place! Right, boys?"

"Yes, ma'am!" we said in fear and unison.

"It might not feel like we are that close to catching the bad guys, but we wouldn't even be this close if it weren't for you three thinking on your feet.

I'm quite proud of you and very glad you're safe." Coleman had a genuine smile on his face. "Is there anything I can do for you guys?"

The question sort of surprised me. I didn't really know whether to say, "No, thanks," or ask for some sort of medal.

Scooter spoke up, though. "Yes, sir. Can you keep a lookout for my backpack? I dropped it somewhere in that house."

"You bet, Scooter," he replied, "but I am pretty sure we didn't find a backpack in that house. It might be gone for good. I hope it didn't have anything too valuable in it?"

"No, sir. Just sentimental value. I had a couple walkie-talkies, some gloves, a flashlight, and a—" He paused mid-sentence as if a thought had just hit him.

"And a what?" Coleman asked, pulling a little notebook out of his pocket.

Scooter shook off his thought. "And, uh, a couple of little inventions I have been working on." He said this with an insincere smile. I have been best friends with Scooter for a long time, and I know that he had just figured out something, probably something related to the case. I wondered what it could be and why he didn't want to share it with the Commander.

"Okay, then," he said. "What does it look like?"

"It's all black except for a patch on the front. It's a white soccer ball with 'WARRIORS' written across it. It's from our soccer team."

"Okay." Coleman made a note in his notebook and put it back in his pocket. "I will keep an eye out for that backpack, then." He waved goodbye and then turned around and grabbed the doorknob of the front door. During the entire conversation, he had never moved out of arm's reach of it.

"Goodnight, all," he said as he opened the door and stepped out.

"Goodnight," said almost everyone in return as the front door closed.

CHAPTER 19

But Wait, There's More!

AJ, Scooter, and their families left shortly after Commander Coleman. I talked with my parents for a while and then sat on the couch and zoned out in front of the TV. I honestly don't even remember what was showing. Finally, around ten o'clock, my mom snapped me out of my daze and told me to go get some real rest in my bed. I gave her an extra-long hug and then went straight to bed.

I woke up at noon the next day. I might have even slept longer if my mom hadn't entered my room to drop off some clean laundry. I sat up when I heard her open the creaky door to my closet.

"Well, good morning, darling," she said when she noticed I had woken.

"Hi," I said with an extra-groggy voice.

"Please call Scooter. He has called here at least four times this morning. I told him I would not wake you up to take a phone call."

"Um, thanks," I mumbled.

She left my room and returned a moment later with the house phone. She handed it to me and then shut the door as she walked out.

I first called Scooter's house, but Mrs. Parks said that he was outside somewhere. I knew what that meant. I hung up and then called HQ directly.

Scooter could hardly contain himself when he answered the phone. "Hey, Ty, you have to get down here right away! We have a *really* good lead on where A.F. might be!"

"Really?" I asked suspiciously. I couldn't think of anything that had happened in the last couple days that would help us locate A.F. Maybe Jerry had thought of something else useful and called Scooter to share. Maybe.

"Just get down here, sleepy-head!" he said and hung up.

I held the phone out and looked at it as if to say, "I can't believe you hung up on me!"

Although I was very hungry, I did not stick around the house to eat a proper breakfast (or was it lunch?). I grabbed a banana out of the bowl on the kitchen table and planned on eating it on the way over to Scooter's house. That wouldn't be enough to fill me up, but I figured I could add to it with the junk we had stocked in the fridge in HQ. At the very least, I could eat a pudding cup.

"Bye, Mom! I am headed over to Scooter's house. I guess he is all excited to show me something," I yelled at her as she vacuumed the living room.

"What? Already?" she yelled, then realized she could turn off the vacuum. "Tyler, yesterday you were locked up in a cage! Don't you think it is too soon?"

"Too soon for what?"

"I don't know. I thought you would relax for a while."

"Mom, it's just Scooter's house. It's not like I'm going to the zoo or anything! I already have all my required tiger sightings for this year." I laughed. She didn't.

"I am just going to Scooter's house. I will not go anywhere else without asking you first," I promised. I waited for her to respond.

She shook her head in surrender and turned the vacuum back on. I laughed to myself as I went through the front door and started my walk to Scooter's house.

"Finally! It's about time you showed up!" It was AJ, whining the second I walked into HQ.

"What? I was a little tired," I said as I plopped myself down on the couch. "Plus, I'm sure you already talked about everything without me."

"Yeah, I wish!" AJ said in response. "Scooter made me wait until you got here to spill the beans."

I laughed. "Okay, well, I'm here now. So how did you figure out where A.F. is?"

"He is with my backpack," Scooter said with a knowing smile. I hate it when he does that.

"I thought you lost your backpack when you were kidnapped," AJ said, confused.

"Yep, that is what I said." Scooter said, still wearing that smirk on his face.

"Then why would A.F. have it now? I don't get it." AJ threw his hands up in frustration.

"Are you saying A.F. is one of the kidnappers?" I asked.

"That is exactly what I am saying," Scooter replied.

"Why would you think that A.F. is one of the kidnappers? I thought A.F. was just messing with us by sending us on a wild goose chase of following Jerry around town."

That's what I thought at first too, but as I thought more about it, I began to ask myself, 'Why would A.F. send us on a wild goose chase?' He had to have a reason."

"He just enjoys messing with us," AJ said.

"Then why send Jerry around town doing weird stuff too?"

"I don't know. Why does A.F. do any of the things he does?" AJ said in frustration.

"Exactly!" Scooter said, satisfied.

"Good! Huh, wait, you didn't answer my question," AJ said, still confused.

I had to admit, I felt just like AJ—completely clueless as to what Scooter was trying to say.

"Let me back up," Scooter began. "As I was trying to figure all of this out, I thought, 'Why does A.F. do anything?' The answer is not because he likes messing with us. It is because he is up to no good. So then why would he send Jerry around to do weird things in town? And why send us around to follow him?" He paused as if he wanted us to answer.

"Because he is up to no good?" AJ offered.

"Exactly!" Scooter said. "And why would his being up to no good require us and Jerry to be running around town for no real reason?"

I started to put things together as he was explaining. "Because he needed us out of the way!"

"Exactly!" Scooter said, getting excited. "Do you realize that the day after we visited the old Safari House is the day that we were hired by A.F. to follow Jerry around? I don't think that was a coincidence. I think A.F. was in the middle of using that house to store exotic animals, and he must have seen us that day. He had to think of a way to keep us distracted and keep us away."

"So why did he eventually tell us that he was just messing with us?" I asked. He had a good theory; I was just trying to find a problem with it.

"Did you notice there were at least three cages in that house? Maybe he just had to keep us distracted long enough that he could sell whatever was in those other cages. Or maybe he thought that he had distracted us long enough for us to lose interest in whatever we were looking for at the old Safari House."

"Anyway, I was wondering what Jerry had to do

with all this, so I called him to ask what he had been doing the day before he was 'hired' by A.F. posing as the CIA. And you know what he said?"

"He was at the yogurt shop, pretending to be a spy," AJ joked.

"Actually, yes," Scooter laughed. "But he said he also spent some time up at the old Safari House, reading the new spy novel he had picked up at the library! I think A.F. must have seen him at the Safari House and decided he could kill two birds with one stone. He would hire Jerry as a spy, and he would hire us to go looking for him. And that would keep all of us busy and away from the Safari House, where they were smuggling animals."

"Well, it sounds like a great theory, but even if it's true, that doesn't put us any closer to catching A.F., now, does it?" I said.

"Not so fast," Scooter said with a smile. "It actually does."

"How?" AJ said excitedly.

"How did you find us yesterday, AJ?" Scooter asked.

"I already told you. I used your computer to locate the tracker that you already had in your pocket."

"Yes, you did. And that is how we are going to find A.F. too."

"He has a tracker in his pocket?" AJ asked.

"No, silly. But remember when Commander Coleman asked what was in my backpack that was worth anything? Well, I couldn't tell him at the time, but I remembered that I had a few extra trackers in there just in case."

"I knew it," I interrupted. "I could tell yesterday that you had realized something, and you weren't going to share."

"Guilty as charged," he said sheepishly. "Anyway, so last night I came down here to see if the trackers had moved from the old Safari House, where I had last seen my backpack." He paused for dramatic effect.

"And?" AJ asked impatiently.

"Yeah, don't leave us hanging like that, Scoot," I said.

Scooter unfolded a piece of paper he had printed out the night before. It was a printed map showing results from his tracking software. "So here is the old Safari House. You can see the tracker was there for a while two days ago. Then, look, it started moving north. It went past our neighborhood and kept going all the way up to here." He pointed toward the top of the map. "It looks like my backpack has been sitting right there ever since."

"Where is that? That looks like it's quite a long way from here," I observed.

"It is. That is almost ten miles north of here. There is nothing up that way but a bunch of farmland."

"I was going to say, 'Let's go check it out,' but ten miles is a little far for an afternoon bike ride!" AJ said.

"I was thinking the same thing, which is why I

already talked to Jimmy, who said he is willing to drive us up there as long as we wash his car for him." Jimmy Langsworth lived next door to Scooter. He owned a very nice Camaro that he liked to show off any chance he got. This would not be one of those times. We were asking him to drive us up into the middle of farm country. There wouldn't be anyone to impress up there.

"Sounds good to me," AJ said. "It's hot enough out, I wouldn't mind getting a little wet! So when are we going?"

"Jimmy said anytime we want. He is just hanging out in his garage, listening to his radio," Scooter answered. "And one more thing: we have to go pick up Jerry. He is coming with us."

"Why are we taking him with us?" I asked.

"Because we need him to identify the man who hired him to be a spy. If my theory is right, and A.F. is behind this, then we should find A.F. when we find the backpack."

"Okay, fine," I said. "But it's going to be a little cramped in Jimmy's back seat. And you know I have to ride in the front, or else I'll get sick."

"Yeah, yeah, we know," AJ said. "At least it's only ten miles."

"Oh, and I have to call my mom first. I promised I wouldn't go anywhere else without asking first. She is still a little freaked out. You know, tigers and all," I laughed.

"Okay, but hurry," Scooter said.

I went over and picked up the HQ phone and dialed home. My mother answered after a couple rings. "Hey, Mom, I have good news. We know where Scooter's backpack is."

"That's great, Tyler! I'm surprised that Commander Coleman found it so quickly. Scooter is probably very excited."

"He is; he is. Anyway, I'm wondering if it would be okay if we go get it. Scooter's neighbor said he would drive us."

"Okay, I think that will be fine. Just be back by dinner at six, okay?"

"Yes, ma'am," I said with a smile. "Love you, Mom." And I hung up.

I turned around to see AJ and Scooter staring with mouths wide open.

"What?" I asked.

"Did you just lie to her?" AJ asked in astonishment.

"I did not say anything that was not true," I stated matter-of-factly. "We are going to go get Scooter's backpack, aren't we?"

"Yeah, but—"

"But what?" I interrupted AJ.

"I think that is going to come back to bite you," Scooter said as he stood up and headed toward the vault door.

"Nah," I said as I followed him out of HQ.

CHAPTER 20
Road Trip to Nowhere

Jimmy was very excited to give us a ride because he was even more excited about getting his car washed. I am not sure why—the thing was practically spotless as it was. It seemed like every time I turned around, Jimmy was in his driveway, washing or waxing his fiery red Camaro.

Despite AJ's protests, he and Scooter hopped in the back seat, and I took the front as we took the relatively short car ride down the hill to pick up Jerry.

Jerry was waiting out front with his now-famous backpack sitting in his lap. He jumped up when the red Camaro pulled into his driveway. I got out so he could get in the back, and after a little whining and pushing and shoving and complaining, we were all inside the car and off on our short road trip.

"AJ, you have your cell phone, right?" Scooter asked.

"Of course. Can't get away from this thing now." He patted his shorts pocket, where the phone was safely tucked away.

"Okay, cool. Say, Jimmy, can you drop us off, and then we will call you in a couple hours to come pick us back up if we need it."

Jimmy just gave a nod. Jimmy didn't tend to say much.

"Okay, cool," Scooter said as we continued driving north. "We should be coming up on the turn shortly."

From his spot in the middle of the back seat, Scooter referenced his printout map and gave directions on when and where to turn, until he finally told Jimmy that this was the spot. Jimmy gave Scooter a confused look. We were kind of in the middle of nowhere.

"Yeah, I know, there is not much out here, but this is really the spot," he told Jimmy with a smile.

Since we were on some deserted back road, Jimmy just stopped the car right in the middle of the road, and we all piled out. AJ, Jerry, and I looked around in confusion while Scooter waved for Jimmy to leave. Jimmy hesitantly pulled away and then finally decided the straight road was a great excuse to speed up and test his new tires. They screeched in protest as he sped away.

We looked around at the farmland that surrounded us. Trees and bushes separated the various fields and lined the country roads that crisscrossed here and there.

"This is really the spot, huh?" AJ asked skeptically.

"Well, sort of. As you know, the tracker only

narrows down the location so far." He pointed to a barn way off in the distance. "I am guessing my backpack is in that barn. It is the only building anywhere close to where the software says my tracker could be. It is either there, or my backpack is out in the middle of one of these fields."

Jerry spoke up. "Wait, so tell me more about these tracker things."

Scooter's face said that he realized he had said too much in front of Jerry.

I guessed it wouldn't hurt to come clean now, so I spoke up. "Well, Scooter made these little tracking devices using GPS from old cell phones. We use them all the time. That's actually how we were able to follow you this week. We stuck one to your bicycle seat. At Scooter's house, he has a computer that tracks when and where the device moves."

"Oh, you guys are good," Jerry marveled. "Are you sure you're not junior spies?"

"Nope, just smart," AJ said proudly. "That's how I found you guys in that basement. Scooter had put one of those trackers in his pocket, and all of us forgot about it for a while."

"Couldn't you have remembered a little sooner?" Jerry joked.

"Sorry about that," AJ said, and we all laughed.

"Anyway, moving on," Scooter continued. "The bad guys stole my backpack when they stuck us in that cage, and I just so happened to have a couple of those trackers tucked away in that backpack.

The software I designed says the trackers must be around here. So I am guessing the backpack is in that barn over there."

"Well, come on, let's go," AJ said as he started walking down the road.

"Hey, wait! We can't just walk right up there. We have to stake things out first." It was Jerry.

"We can't really do that from here, now, can we?" AJ snapped back.

"Actually, we can," Jerry said as he set his backpack on the ground and unzipped the top. He pulled out a pair of binoculars with a weird antenna sticking out from the top.

"Binoculars! Of course. Very nice!" AJ admired.

"Those aren't just binoculars. Those are GX-500 PP5 Binoculars with night-vision capabilities, telescoping lenses, electronic compass, and GPS redirect," Jerry said proudly.

"Whoa," AJ said. "What else did you bring?"

Jerry started pulling out a bunch of other gadgets, walkie-talkies, earpieces, collar microphones to attach to your shirt, road flares, and other stuff I had no clue about but looked really expensive. If I didn't know better, I would think Jerry really was a spy.

Of course, Scooter was the most interested in all the cool spy toys. "Where did you get this stuff?" he marveled.

"I thought I told you, I have a subscription to *Spy Weekly*. I ordered all this stuff from their catalog.

And at a discount too."

"Well, I guess you were ready for this moment, huh?" I joked.

"Tyler, I was born for this moment." He grabbed the binoculars and looked toward the barn. AJ, Scooter, and I waited quietly as he looked in the binoculars and whispered to himself under his breath. He began to fumble with the buttons on the binoculars and seemed to be getting frustrated with them. Finally, he spoke up. "I don't see anything suspicious over by the barn, but I can't seem to get these things to zoom in at all."

Scooter walked over and stuck out his hand. "May I?"

Jerry handed him the binoculars.

Scooter gave it a quick glance and said. "It says you have to add batteries to work the zoom function. Did you do that?"

"Really? No, I didn't know that. This is my first time to get to use all this stuff."

AJ rolled his eyes. He was suddenly not as impressed as he had been just a moment ago.

Scooter helped Jerry out. "Well, hey, no big deal. The binoculars will still work even if we can't zoom."

Scooter helped Jerry put all the stuff back in his bag. Jerry was becoming more dejected by the minute. With each item he put back in his backpack, he realized he had no clue how it worked.

It didn't take binoculars to see how hard it would be to approach the barn. The only thing directly between us and the barn was a huge field of some green crop that wasn't mature enough to tell what it was. On the left side of the field was a dirt road that went from the road we were standing on, ran along the edge of the field, passed the left side of the barn, and circled behind it. The road looked to be rarely used. It consisted of two dirt tracks running side by side, with a patch of grass and weeds growing in between. Even farther to our left was a line of trees and sporadic bushes that ran along the entire length of the road. We could see tall trees rising above the roof of the barn, so it appeared as if there was quite a bit of woods near the barn. If we could ever get there.

When they had everything but the binoculars packed away, Scooter spoke up. "So see this tree line over on the left? I think we use that for cover and work our way to those woods behind the barn. Then we figure out what to do from there."

We all agreed and followed behind Scooter as we worked our way toward the barn. It took us almost a half hour to reach the woods behind the barn. It is amazing how slow you have to go when you're trying not to be seen and you have to stop every few feet and re-check that no one is watching you.

We sat in a grove of trees about 50 feet behind the barn and tried to catch our breath. The barn that had looked so small when we were far away now towered above us. We had not seen it before while looking in the binoculars, but there was an old green pickup parked behind the barn. It had a large, empty cage in the back. Next to the truck was a small back door to the barn, and it was propped halfway open. The door opened toward us so we couldn't see the doorway behind it.

AJ was about to speak when Scooter shushed him and whispered, "Listen."

We sat silently for a minute and soon could hear what Scooter must have heard. At first it sounded like growling, and then you could hear hissing, and then came the distinct cackling of monkeys!

"You hear that?" AJ whispered. "They got monkeys in there!"

"They must have moved all the animals out of the Safari House to this barn," I said.

"That makes perfect sense," Scooter added. "With the nearest house miles away, these animals can make all the noise they want, and no one will hear them. This is the perfect place to hold them. This must be why A.F. sent us on a wild goose chase, so they would have time to move all the animals out here while we were not around."

"So what do we do now?" I asked. "Don't you think it is about time we call Commander Coleman and tell him we located the kidnappers?"

"We will in a second," he argued. "But first, I think we need to do a little info-gathering. We are not really sure what we are dealing with. How many guys are inside? What animals do they have?

I heard some monkeys and maybe another tiger, but what else might be in there? He should know that so he knows what sort of reinforcements to bring with him. I think we are safe in our little hideout for now." Of course, these words would come back to haunt all of us, like many of the things that Scooter says.

Just then a man walked out of the open back door and went over to the truck. The four of us crouched even lower in the bushes and then froze. The man opened the passenger-side door of the truck and pulled out some rope. He then shut the door and began to take advantage of the open air to do some stretches. He had probably been sitting for a long time and welcomed the break. The man was tall and had short, dark hair. He was also very muscular. From what I remembered, this man fit the description of the CIA agent who had come to Jerry's door. I would have loved to lean over to Jerry and ask if that was the guy, but I didn't dare move. I just kept my eyes on the man as he twisted and turned to try and stay loose. Could I really be looking at *the* A.F.? After all the mystery, here he was, standing right in front of us, and he didn't even know we were watching!

The man stretched for another minute or two and then took the rope he had come outside to get and went back inside the barn. I immediately turned to Jerry. So did Scooter and AJ. We all basically asked in unison, "Was that the guy? Was that the man who came to your door, pretending to be from the CIA?"

"That's him," Jerry said confidently.

"We have him," Scooter said with a satisfying smile.

"Sweet! Solved the case and the A.F. mystery at the same time," AJ said. "How long do you think it will take Commander Coleman to get out here, anyway?"

"Hold up. We need more information first," Scooter said. "Did you guys see what I saw when A.F. opened the truck door?"

"Probably not," I said, rolling my eyes.

"When he opened the door, there was a moment when the side mirror was at just the right angle, and I could actually see inside the barn. It was too fast to make anything out, but I think I could see another guy and a cage."

"Yeah, so?" AJ said.

"So, it's pretty risky, but if one of us could get over there and turn the mirror just a little bit, we would actually be able to stay right here in our hiding spot and still see everything going on inside. We could gather info for a few minutes and then call the police with that much more information!"

"I'll do it!" Jerry said. He stood up.

"Jerry, I can't ask you to do that. This is my crazy idea."

"Nonsense," he said, walking out of the woods, leaving his backpack with us. "Like I said, I have been training for something like this my whole life."

Scooter wanted to continue to argue, but Jerry was already far enough away that Scooter would have had to yell at him to do so. We all watched nervously as Jerry quickly made his way over to the back wall of the barn. He put his back against the building and then slowly shuffled toward the open door and the truck. When he got to the door, he looked through the crack where the door was attached to the barn by two hinges. He stared for a few minutes. I am guessing he was gathering as much information as he could, as well as looking for an opportunity to step over to the truck and start messing with the mirror. When he moved to the mirror, he would be completely out in the open—then he would be most in danger of getting caught.

Finally, he must have thought it was the right time. He started to inch his way out into the open and toward the truck. The three of us in the woods held our breath as we watched.

As he neared the truck, we heard a rumbling sound coming from our right. I turned to see a large moving truck rumbling down the driveway toward us! I looked back at Jerry. He was too focused on what he was doing to look in our direction. He just kept moving toward the truck. I guess sound bounced around the barn in such a way that Jerry couldn't hear the truck rolling down the driveway. He had no clue that in a few seconds the truck would be coming around the corner, and he would be caught! It didn't matter, though. Even if he did hear the truck, at this point, he had nowhere to run. If he tried running back over to us in the bushes, he would have to run across the driveway and right in front of the truck, and he couldn't run the opposite direction because he would have to run in front of the open barn door.

I felt so helpless as I watched Jerry's fate become more sealed with every passing second.

As the truck neared the corner of the barn, it was clear that Jerry could now hear it. He stopped his slow approach toward the truck and looked around for a place to hide, but there was none! I saw him panic, and then I lost sight of him as the large truck drove in front of us and blocked my view.

CHAPTER 21

A Not-So-Perfect Look Inside the Barn

The truck pulled up next to the green truck that was already parked there. I could now see the barn door again, but Jerry was nowhere to be seen! A short, balding man climbed out of the passenger side of the truck that had just arrived. He was wearing a dark blue suit with a crisp, white shirt and a bright red tie. He looked down in disgust at his black dress shoes, which were not as shiny as they had been before walking on the dusty driveway. The driver of the truck left the loud motor running and walked around the front of the truck. He was a tall man wearing coveralls and a very dirty baseball cap. I guessed that the man in the suit was the boss, and the driver was the employee doing all the dirty work.

Just then A.F. and another man walked out of the barn to greet their guests. The man with A.F. was not nearly as tall or as muscular as him, but he looked like he had done his fair share of hard work in his life. The four men shook hands and smiled and then began to talk. I assumed they were talking business, but I couldn't actually hear anything because they were over 50 feet away and the noise from the truck engine was drowning them out. As I watched the four talk, I began to wonder just what had happened to Jerry. Clearly, he had not been caught yet. I looked around for where he may have disappeared to. There really weren't many places for him to go!

Then I saw him: he was laying on the ground underneath the green truck! He must have hit the dirt and rolled underneath the parked vehicle at the same time that the other truck had come around the corner. I can only imagine how he must have felt at that moment. He could see four sets of shoes shuffling in place, only a few feet from his head!

The meeting of the four men broke up, and the two from the barn went back inside. The man in the suit went to get something out of the truck, and the driver of the truck went to the back of the truck and rolled up the back door. From our vantage point, we could easily see inside. It was completely empty except for a small cage. I wondered what sort of animal would go in a cage that small, but I didn't have to wonder very long.

A.F. and his partner came back out of the barn, each carrying opposite ends of a cage. Inside the cage was a young tiger. The tiger was about the size of a golden retriever. I wondered if the tiger back at the Safari House might be this smaller tiger's parent. I would have said it was cute, except for the fact that it was hissing and snarling at the two men as they carried it toward the back of the truck. They put the cage into the back of the truck, and then they both climbed inside as well. They were joined by the driver of the truck. The three men spent the next couple minutes trying to convince the tiger to leave one cage and enter the other. Eventually, they succeeded. They all got out, and the driver pulled the rolling door back down. A.F. went over to the man in the suit, and the rich man handed him a bag. I assumed the bag was full of cash—probably payment for his new pet tiger.

The driver hopped back in the truck, and after a handshake with A.F., the man in the suit got back in as well. The truck quickly pulled away, and A.F. and his partner sat on the now-empty cage they had brought out. They were probably enjoying a moment of fresh air. Believe me, you don't know how much you miss it until you don't have it.

What happened next, I can only describe as ridiculous—and yet predictable. With all that has happened with this case, I should have seen this coming.

We sat as still as possible in the woods, watching the men with their backs to us. Now that the noisy truck was gone, the afternoon seemed to demand quiet. Which made it that much more disturbing when AJ's phone started singing! AJ quickly fumbled in his pocket, trying to turn the ringer off. It was too late, though, the two men turned around with confused looks on their faces. They stood up and started to walk toward the woods we were hiding in. I'm sure Scooter would have loved to give a lecture to AJ about the importance of putting his phone on silent, but there was no time. There wasn't even enough time to give dirty looks!

Instead, he jumped up and said, "Run!" and started to run down the driveway. AJ and I jumped up and followed him. The two men took off, running after us.

I wish we had thought about this earlier: with three of us and only two men chasing us, if we had just run different directions, it would have been impossible to catch all three of us. But at that moment, I wasn't doing much thinking. The only thought I had was to catch up with Scooter and hope I could outrun the adults. It was a lousy plan.

AJ quickly took the lead and kept on sprinting down the long, dirt driveway toward the paved road. About the time I caught up to Scooter, both of us were tackled by the man who was not A.F. "I got these two" is all he said as A.F. continued running after AJ. AJ is fast, very fast. But he was no match for the tall, athletic A.F. The adult's stride was so much bigger than AJ's that he caught him in no time. He didn't even have to tackle AJ; he was running fast enough that as he pulled up even with AJ,

AJ decided it wasn't worth the fight and just stopped running. A.F. wrapped a large hand around AJ's arm and forcefully walked him back down the driveway toward us.

The two men forced us to walk back to the barn and around to the backside. When we came around the corner, I could see that Jerry was gone from his hiding spot under the green truck. Good. I guess he had managed to get out while we were being chased. I sort of wondered if he had found a safe hiding spot and if he had any clue where to go to find help. I didn't have much time to think about it, though. I had problems of my own. The men muscled us through the back door of the barn, and as you probably can guess, they threw all three of us into an empty cage and wrestled the door shut.

"There you go. Sorry this one ain't as roomy as the last one," the man who was not A.F. said as he locked the cage door with a padlock.

Not many people can claim they have been locked in a cage before. I can unfortunately say that I have been twice! In the same week! Like the man had said, this cage was not nearly as roomy as the one at the Safari House. It was cramped, and the three of us spent the first minute or two just trying to get comfortable without kicking each other in the face. We finally managed to all get seated and facing out toward the rest of the barn.

The other animals were all growling and cawing and howling with excitement to see new creatures they were not familiar with. My view was partially blocked by stacks of boxes next to our cage, but I could see there was an alligator—or was it a crocodile? I don't know; I still can't keep them straight. Anyway, there were also some colorful birds, a couple monkeys, some sort of deer with weird horns, and another full-grown tiger. This one was completely black-and-white, without a trace of orange, unlike the one we had seen back at the Safari House.

Although it was still very light outside, there were no windows in the barn to let the light in. It would have been very dark inside if not for two camping lanterns. One was hanging from a rope in the middle of the barn, and the other was sitting on a table that the men had made out of some old wood. A.F. was sitting at the table, a pile of papers spread out in front of him. He was mumbling something to himself.

"What do you think A.F. is going to do to us?" I whispered to the others.

"I don't think that is A.F.," Scooter whispered back.

"What do you mean? Jerry said that's the guy who came to his house and hired him to be a fake CIA agent. I thought you said he did that to keep us away from the Safari House."

"Oh, I believe A.F. is behind all this," Scooter replied. "I just don't think either of these guys is A.F."

"What makes you say that?" AJ jumped in.

"For starters, the guy who knocked on Jerry's door has not said a single word to us. Does that sound like A.F.? A.F. likes to taunt us every chance he gets. This guy seems like he doesn't have any clue what he wants to do with us. And the other guy is taking orders from the tall guy. Do you see A.F. taking orders from anyone? A.F. seems like he would need to be in charge."

"You're probably right," I said with resignation. "Man, I thought we finally figured out who we were dealing with."

CHAPTER 22
Surviving on Dog Food

The shorter man was pacing in the middle of the barn. He hollered at his partner, "Man, there is no way I can take a whole nother week holed up in this place. I'm going to go crazy!"

"That's okay. The boss says he had to move up the time table. We gotta be done in two days, tops."

"What? When did you talk to the boss?"

"I didn't. He left us a note. He must have stopped by here this morning, while we were out making that delivery."

Scooter and I gave each other a knowing look at the mention of the boss.

"Well, did he say anything else?" the shorter man asked.

"Just that if we manage to meet the new delivery deadline, he would wire us an extra ten grand."

"Nice!"

"Yeah. And I almost forgot. He also left us a battery-powered TV to fight the boredom while we wait." The tall guy pointed to a stack of hay bales in the corner. There was a small TV sitting on top of them. And next to the TV was Scooter's backpack! I waved to get Scooter's attention and pointed. He smiled and nodded.

The shorter man came over to our cage. "So what are we gonna do with these three?"

The taller man answered without even looking up from his paperwork. "Two more days, and we'll have all these animals delivered. I say we just keep them locked up in that cage. They aren't going to cause any more problems while they're in there. They can yell as loud as they want, and no one is going to hear them."

"But what about food?" Of course it was AJ who asked.

"Shut up, kid," the tall man snapped back. "I am not a big fan of yours right now. We had to change a lot of plans because of you three, and I am none too happy about it. There are a ton of places I would rather be, but instead, I'm stuck in a barn, babysitting zoo animals—and now three kids as well!"

"Don't worry, kid, we won't let you starve. We got plenty of dog food for you to snack on!" The short guy laughed as he patted a tall stack of bagged dog food that was sitting next to us. Apparently, that's what the men were feeding the animals while they waited for people to come pick them up.

Scooter decided to pry a little bit more to gain more information about A.F. "So when is the boss coming back?"

The smaller man spoke up. "He ain't coming. He don't like to get his hands dirty."

"Be quiet! Don't talk to them," the taller man snapped at his partner.

Scooter continued, "I would say your boss is not going to be happy about this. I mean, you know how easy it was for a bunch of us kids to find you—not once, but twice? He might start docking your pay. How much is he paying you, anyway?"

"Well, actually—" the shorter man started to answer, but the taller man had come over from his table to stop him from going on.

"I told you not to talk to them! Go feed the alligator."

"Since when are you in charge?" the shorter man argued.

"Since the day you didn't properly close the cages, and you let half these animals loose!" the taller man said. "Now go feed the animals." He shoved the other man to the side of the room that was out of our view.

He turned toward Scooter. "Listen, kid, I get paid to deliver these animals to their new homes, not to put up with any lip from you. Keep your mouth shut for the next couple days, and you will probably get to see your mommy and daddy again. Keep yapping, and you probably won't." He grabbed one of the bars to our cage and gave it one hard shake before he turned and walked back to his paperwork.

Gulp. That was enough motivation to keep me quiet. Obviously not for Scooter, though. He was about to say something else when AJ gave him an elbow in the ribs so hard it actually made Scooter cough. AJ shot him a warning glance that basically said, "Even if that man doesn't hurt you, I will."

We sat there in silence for a few minutes. The taller man received a phone call from someone that sounded like a client. He purposely kept this voice low enough so we couldn't easily make out what he was saying. My legs were already cramping. There was no way I would last a couple hours in this small cage, let alone a couple days. The memories of being stuck in the bigger cage earlier were enough to send me into panic mode. How could we get out?

I had a quick idea. Maybe the next time the tall man was on the phone, we could start making tons of noise. He would have to come over to the cage to threaten us to be quiet. If he got close enough, we could reach through the bars of the cage and grab the phone from him. The cage might be keeping us in, but it was also keeping him out. We could dial 911 long before he could ever get the cage unlocked to retrieve his phone. Nah, that would be way too dangerous! Who knew what the man would do if we made him mad again?

Wait! We have a phone: AJ had a phone! That's what got us into this mess in the first place. I hadn't seen them confiscate the phone when they tossed us in the cage, so AJ must still have it! AJ was on the opposite side of the cage from me, with Scooter in between us. I got AJ's attention and then mouthed the word, "Phone."

AJ looked at me in confusion and mouthed, "What?"

I held my hand up to my head as if I was holding a phone and mouthed the word again.

AJ shook his head *no*.

Scooter leaned over to me and whispered in my ear, "I already asked him about it. He thinks he dropped it out in the woods when he was trying to turn the ringer off."

"Great," I said aloud. It didn't matter if anyone heard that. They couldn't really make it any worse for me.

An hour later, the shorter man came back into view. He had apparently finished his duties of feeding the various animals, and he went over to the table and joined his taller partner. They were both hunched over the table, looking at various pieces of paper and whispering so we wouldn't hear. We must have been the topic of conversation because they both looked our direction every couple seconds. Finally, the taller man said something that ended in "no loose ends." The shorter man started to walk toward our cage with a determined and menacing look. We were pretty squished in our cage, but I still instinctively tried to back away from the front of the cage.

Suddenly, I heard a familiar voice: "Freeze! Both

of you! This is the police. Put your hands above your head."

I could not see the doorway where the police were standing, but I would recognize that voice anywhere. It was Commander Coleman! The two men slowly raised their hands above their heads as a bunch of police officers swarmed into the room and immediately put them in handcuffs. Commander Coleman walked into the room and marveled at all the animals in their cages. He scanned the room until he came to our cage, and then he let out a huge, bellowing laugh.

"You guys didn't have enough fun last time you were locked up, huh? Decided to try it again?" He laughed even louder the second time.

"Just get us out of here," I begged.

"I should really take a picture first," he joked as he walked away from us, toward the police officers who were questioning the two men. I was a little worried that Commander Coleman was actually serious and that he was looking for someone with a camera, but he came back in a minute with a handful of keys and started trying to find which one fit the lock. Apparently, he had gotten the kidnappers to cooperate and hand over the set of keys.

"Boys, I thought you told me there was nothing else you could share with me to add to this case," he said as he tried each key in the lock. It seemed sort of weird to be having a conversation with someone while locked in a cage.

Scooter spoke up. "We were going to call you once we knew what we were dealing with."

"I'm not buying it," the Commander said with a frown.

"Seriously, we were about to call you, but then everything went haywire," AJ jumped in to Scooter's defense.

"Boys, you can't—" He stopped himself mid-sentence. He took a deep breath and then started again. "We will have a long talk when we get down to the station. You want to be the heroes, but this makes one too many close calls."

"But—" Scooter was intent on arguing, but the Commander held up his hand and stopped him.

"Enough" is the only word he spoke as he finally found the correct key and unlocked the cage. We all climbed out and immediately starting stretching in the middle of the barn. We had only been trapped in the cage for an hour or so, but every muscle in my body seemed to be cramping in protest.

We then followed Coleman out the back door, where we found Jerry leaning against a police car. When he saw all three of us still in one piece, a big smile came across his face.

"I see you didn't become tiger food," he joked. He dug a phone out of his pocket and handed it to AJ. "I believe you dropped this. And you might want to call your mom back; she has called like six times already." Three of us laughed. AJ just groaned.

"Where did you find this?" AJ asked. "Is this

how the police found us? You called them from my phone, didn't you?"

Jerry attempted to answer all of his questions with one story. "Yeah, after your phone started ringing and those dudes started walking toward you, I saw you drop the phone in those bushes over there." He pointed to our previous hiding spot. "Once they started chasing after you down the road, I scrambled out from underneath the truck and found a new hiding spot in the bushes. After they took you guys inside, I slowly worked my way through the woods back to where we had been hiding. I was hoping my backpack would still be where I had left it. Once I got back to our spot, it didn't take me long to find your phone. It was right next to my backpack. I called the police but had no clue where we are—I still don't—so it took the police a little while to figure out where I was calling from. And the rest is obviously history."

"Well, thanks, dude!" AJ said. "If it weren't for you, we would have been eating dog food for the next two days."

Commander Coleman had Scooter, Tyler, and me pile into the back of his police car and asked that another officer take Jerry home. He said something about Jerry's record being not quite as long. The Commander told us to sit tight, and then he went back inside the barn. I looked around the back seat and realized that I was becoming all too familiar with the back of Commander Coleman's car. I looked forward and took note of the bars that separated the back seat from the front. Once again, it looked like I was in a cage. I chuckled to myself. Three cages in less than a week—that might just be some sort of record.

Commander Coleman came back out of the barn a few minutes later, and he was carrying Scooter's backpack. He opened the car door and said, "Is this yours?"

Scooter nodded. Coleman just tossed the backpack on Scooter's lap and shut the door without saying a word.

Epilogue

On the way to the police station, AJ decided to call his mother back, and even without having the phone on speaker, we could hear her yelling at AJ. Not the most pleasant conversation to listen to. And I'm sure if you asked AJ, he would say not that much fun to be part of, either. I would find out myself soon enough.

First, we all got an earful from Commander Coleman down at the police station. To summarize, he said that the Enigma Squad and Commander Coleman should share things on a need-to-know basis—and he "needed to know" everything! While he was grateful for our help in solving the case, he was getting really tired of us withholding valuable clues from him, Scooter especially.

Unfortunately, that was the relatively pain-free lecture. When I got home, I got the painful one. My mom was absolutely furious with me for lying to her. Once again, I tried to explain to her that I did not say anything to her that was not true. That was probably a mistake. She must have lectured me for ten minutes before she got tired and left my room in frustration. When she returned, my dad was with her, and that is when I knew I was in real hot water. My dad tends to be a little less "excitable" than my mom, but he just has a way of putting things so they tend to sink in better. Maybe it's a man-to-man thing; I don't know.

Anyway, he said a bunch of stuff, but the thing that is still ringing in my head is when he looked right into my eyes and said, "Son, if you allow someone to come to the wrong conclusion, it doesn't matter if they jumped there or you pushed them, it's still lying."

At that moment I think it really did start to sink in, but Mom and Dad wanted to make sure. So as you can probably guess, they grounded me to my room for another two weeks. Man, I feel like I have been spending my whole summer in my room! I at least made good use of the time and put together this case file while I had nothing better to do.

Well, fortunately, my parents did not send me to my room immediately. I was given one last chance to see Scooter and AJ before being barred from seeing them for the next two weeks. In light of our recent kidnapping and then rescue, Mrs. Parks decided to throw an impromptu party at her house that evening to celebrate our safe return. She invited all of AJ's family and all of mine. She even invited Jerry and his family to join us, but they politely declined. They decided to get out of town for a few days and avoid any further excitement.

So this little get together was the last chance I was going to get to see AJ and Scooter for a couple weeks. And it did not start out very well. All the adults wanted to do was talk. They wanted to know all about our little adventures, and how we felt, and what the tiger looked like, and a bunch of other questions we didn't feel like answering. Finally, the adults changed the conversation to the recent news and began to forget that we boys were in the room. We took that as a good excuse to escape to Scooter's room.

When we got upstairs, the first thing we did was compare punishments. Of course I had the most severe of the three.

"Of course your punishment is going to be the worst," Scooter scolded. "We didn't flat-out lie to our parents!"

"Yeah, but you lied to the police," I countered.

"Yeah, and I got a week in my room for it!" Scooter complained.

AJ had gotten the lightest sentence of all of us. His parents told him he had to stay home for three days for "acting like a fool." Those were the words they used. AJ then had the nerve to whine because he had to wash Jimmy's car by himself since Scooter and I would still be grounded.

I then told the boys that I planned on spending my time putting together the case file for *The Case of the Tiger on the Toilet*. The catchy title was my idea, naturally. I asked Scooter if he could get me a printout of the map showing the trackers' movements up to the barn where we caught the kidnappers. He said, "Sure," and jumped on his computer to load up the tracker software.

After a minute he said, "Uh-oh, we have a problem."

"What's the matter?" AJ asked.

"The software must be going wonky. Look at this." He pointed at the screen. "This says that one of the trackers is still very active. Look, it is moving right now, as we speak." We could see one of the bright green dots, moving across a map of Silverdale.

"How long has it been moving? You can check where it's been, right?" I asked.

"Yes, let me get to that screen." He pushed a few buttons and brought up another map. "It looks like that tracker has been moving around various places in Silverdale for the past ten hours. But that is impossible. All the trackers are in my backpack, which is right there." He pointed to his backpack sitting next to his bed.

"Hold on," he said, jumping up from his chair. He reached over, grabbed his backpack, and ripped the zipper open. He tipped the bag over and dumped all the contents onto his bed. That was a bad idea because half the stuff inside was still covered in flour from a few days ago. Scooter didn't care. He frantically rummaged through the various objects, locating the trackers. He stopped and shook his head. In his hand, he held five trackers.

"Yup. One is missing. I put six in my bag." He looked down in disgust at the contents of his bag, sprawled across his bed. We all stared in silence for a moment.

"Wait a minute," Scooter said finally. He reached into the pile of stuff and grabbed a small envelope. "This is not mine!"

He flipped it over. It read *Enigma Squad* in typed letters on the front. He looked up at AJ and me as if we might know what the letter was all about. We just shrugged our shoulders.

He quickly tore the envelope open and unfolded a small note. Again in typed letters, it read:

Enigma Squad,

I must admit I am slightly impressed—but more annoyed. You have freed yourselves and again ruined my plans! You are becoming quite the monkey on my back, and I grow tired of your meddling. Why must you continue to stick your nose where it does not belong?

You want to rattle my cage? Fine. I will give you more than you can handle. I have so many devious plans, you won't be able to keep track. A worthy adversary, you are not! And I will prove it to you. This is not over; I have just begun!

Beware of the ninth, my friends. Beware of the ninth.

A.F.